Critical Acclaim
TRAVELS IN T

"As revelation after revelation
edge, guessing until the very
most intellectually elegant writers. He has persistently subverted
the ordinary mechanisms of suspense, chronology, even genre.…
Themes are hungry ghosts, Borges said. Fortunately, Auster's
ghosts are insatiable."

—Howard Norman, *The Washington Post Book World*

"A novella-length fiction that ruminates on issues of identity, purpose, responsibility, and knowledge in a setting that harks back in
a deliciously retro, knowing sort of way to French existentialist
conventions . . . Readers may choose to read this elegant little
book as an allegory of their country's current predicament, as
writerly conceit, or as wider comment on the modern condition."

—Timothy Rutten, *Los Angeles Times*

"Auster, a literary descendant of Kafka and Borges . . . celebrates
the power of the imagination and marvels over the labyrinthine
nature of the mind in an archly playful and shrewdly philosophi-
cal tribute to the transcendence of stories."

—Donna Seaman, *Booklist*

"Auster's lean, poker-faced prose creates a satisfyingly claustro-
phobic allegory."   —*Publishers Weekly*

"One of America's greats . . . The writing is as tight as ever."

—Jonathan Messinger, *Time Out Chicago*

"This is Auster at his best, giving the reader a protagonist who
knows absolutely nothing about himself, yet is determined to
answer the questions. . . . It stands on its own as another masterly
trip through the mind of one of the most imaginative writers of his
generation."   —Matt Tullis, *The Columbus Dispatch*

MORE . . .

"Cryptic, allusive, revelatory, terrifying, and amusing, the not-to-be-missed *Travels in the Scriptorium* becomes a highly entertaining and wonderfully provocative metaphysical (meta-fictional) meditation on semiotics, epistemology, existence, and literature. . . . Don't let that scare you off from what is one of recent literary history's most fascinating Kafkaesque parables. . . . Don't miss it!" —Bookloons.com

"Mysterious and illusive, Auster's latest novel starts as the haunting story of a nameless old man kept prisoner in a small room and becomes a meditation on the act of creation."
—*Seattle Post-Intelligencer*

"*Travels in the Scriptorium* can be taken as an aestheticized horror story, or as a political parable, and these days, they're really the same thing. It ends with a chilling circularity that suggests a psychotic version of *Groundhog Day*. Like most of Auster's work, it's spare, suggestive, eminently readable, and it doesn't overstay its welcome by a single page." —Scott Eyman, *The Palm Beach Post*

"Auster's bleak gamesmanship again reaps its usual spooky, minimalist rewards. An old man called Mr. Blank wakes up in a sterile furnished room. . . . Who is he? . . . As in other Auster works, the answers—if you can call them that—confound, pleasurably so."
—Gregory Kirschling, *Entertainment Weekly*

"*Travels in the Scriptorium* is, as its author suggests, a small book and Auster has exceeded himself by producing one of his strangest, most labyrinthine works. At times you are almost compelled to make notes to try to piece together the puzzle, to plot an exit or just orient yourself. . . . It's a welcome return to what he does best, and a hauntingly enjoyable read. Trust me."
—Peter Lalor, *The Australian*

"The cool, spooky, parable-like feel is effective."
—*The Sunday Times* (London)

"Ornamented with its clever quirks, fashioned into its intertextual twists and turns . . . Live, mysterious, unfinished, and oddly poignant, it is a fiction in real time; a narrative which, like its protagonist, 'can never die.'" —Belinda McKeon, *The Irish Times*

TRAVELS IN THE SCRIPTORIUM

◆

PAUL AUSTER

PICADOR

HENRY HOLT AND COMPANY
NEW YORK

TRAVELS IN THE SCRIPTORIUM. Copyright © 2006 by Paul Auster. All rights reserved. No part of this book may be used or reproduced in any manner whatsoever without written permission except in the case of brief quotations embodied in critical articles or reviews. For information address Picador, 175 Fifth Avenue, New York, NY, 10010.

Picador® is a U.S. registered trademark and is used by Henry Holt and Company under license from Pan Books Limited.

For information on Picador Reading Group Guides and titles, please contact Picador.
Phone: 1-646-307-5259
Fax: 212-253-9627
E-mail: readinggroupguides@picadorusa.com

ISBN: 0-312-94840-9
EAN: 0-312-94840-5

First published in the United States by Henry Holt and Company.

First Picador Paperback Edition: June 2007

10 9 8 7 6 5 4 3 2 1

for Lloyd Hustvedt
(in memory)

THE OLD MAN SITS on the edge of the narrow bed, palms spread out on his knees, head down, staring at the floor. He has no idea that a camera is planted in the ceiling directly above him. The shutter clicks silently once every second, producing eighty-six thousand four hundred still photos with each revolution of the earth. Even if he knew he was being watched, it wouldn't make any difference. His mind is elsewhere, stranded among the figments in his head as he searches for an answer to the question that haunts him.

Who is he? What is he doing here? When did he arrive

and how long will he remain? With any luck, time will
tell us all. For the moment, our only task is to study the
pictures as attentively as we can and refrain from drawing
any premature conclusions.

There are a number of objects in the room, and on
each one a strip of white tape has been affixed to the surface, bearing a single word written out in block letters.
On the bedside table, for example, the word is TABLE. On
the lamp, the word is LAMP. Even on the wall, which is not
strictly speaking an object, there is a strip of tape that
reads WALL. The old man looks up for a moment, sees the
wall, sees the strip of tape attached to the wall, and pronounces the word *wall* in a soft voice. What cannot be
known at this point is whether he is reading the word on
the strip of tape or simply referring to the wall itself. It
could be that he has forgotten how to read but still recognizes things for what they are and can call them by their
names, or, conversely, that he has lost the ability to recognize things for what they are but still knows how to read.

He is dressed in blue-and-yellow striped cotton pajamas, and his feet are encased in a pair of black leather
slippers. It is unclear to him exactly where he is. In the
room, yes, but in what building is the room located? In a
house? In a hospital? In a prison? He can't remember
how long he has been here or the nature of the circumstances that precipitated his removal to this place. Perhaps he has always been here; perhaps this is where he
has lived since the day he was born. What he knows is
that his heart is filled with an implacable sense of guilt.
At the same time, he can't escape the feeling that he is the
victim of a terrible injustice.

There is one window in the room, but the shade is
drawn, and as far as he can remember he has not yet
looked out of it. Likewise with the door and its white
porcelain knob. Is he locked in, or is he free to come and

go as he wishes? He has yet to investigate this matter—
for, as stated in the first paragraph above, his mind is elsewhere, adrift in the past as he wanders among the
phantom beings that clutter his head, struggling to answer
the question that haunts him.

The pictures do not lie, but neither do they tell the
whole story. They are merely a record of time passing, the
outward evidence. The old man's age, for example, is difficult to determine from the slightly out-of-focus black-
and-white images. The only fact that can be set down
with any certainty is that he is not young, but the word *old*
is a flexible term and can be used to describe a person
anywhere between sixty and a hundred. We will therefore
drop the epithet *old man* and henceforth refer to the person in the room as Mr. Blank. For the time being, no first
name will be necessary.

Mr. Blank stands up from the bed at last, pauses briefly
to steady his balance, and then shuffles over to the desk at
the other end of the room. He feels tired, as if he has just
woken from a fitful, too short night of sleep, and as the
soles of his slippers scrape along the bare wood floor, he
is reminded of the sound of sandpaper. Far off in the distance, beyond the room, beyond the building in which the
room is located, he hears the faint cry of a bird—perhaps
a crow, perhaps a seagull, he can't tell which.

Mr. Blank lowers his body into the chair at the desk. It
is an exceedingly comfortable chair, he decides, made of
soft brown leather and equipped with broad armrests to
accommodate his elbows and forearms, not to speak of an
invisible spring mechanism that allows him to rock back
and forth at will, which is precisely what he begins to do
the moment he sits down. Rocking back and forth has a
soothing effect on him, and as Mr. Blank continues to indulge in these pleasurable oscillations, he remembers the
rocking horse that sat in his bedroom when he was a

small boy, and then he begins to relive some of the imaginary journeys he used to take on that horse, whose name was Whitey and who, in the young Mr. Blank's mind, was not a wooden object adorned with white paint but a living being, a true horse.

After this brief excursion into his early boyhood, anguish rises up into Mr. Blank's throat again. He says out loud in a weary voice: I mustn't allow this to happen. Then he leans forward to examine the piles of papers and photographs stacked neatly on the surface of the mahogany desk. He takes hold of the pictures first, three dozen eight-by-ten black-and-white portraits of men and women of various ages and races. The photo on top shows a young woman in her early twenties. Her dark hair is cropped short, and there is an intense, troubled look in her eyes as she gazes into the lens. She is standing outdoors in some city, perhaps an Italian or French city, because she happens to be positioned in front of a medieval church, and because the woman is wearing a scarf and a woolen coat, it is safe to assume the picture was taken in winter. Mr. Blank stares into the eyes of the young woman and strains to remember who she is. After twenty seconds or so, he hears himself whisper a single word: Anna. A feeling of overpowering love washes through him. He wonders if Anna isn't someone he was once married to, or if, perhaps, he isn't looking at a picture of his daughter. An instant after thinking these thoughts, he is attacked by a fresh wave of guilt, and he knows that Anna is dead. Even worse, he suspects that he is responsible for her death. It might even be, he tells himself, that he was the person who killed her.

Mr. Blank groans in pain. Looking at the pictures is too much for him, so he pushes them aside and turns his attention to the papers. There are four piles in all, each about six inches high. For no particular reason that he is aware of, he reaches for the top page on the pile farthest to the left. The handwritten words, printed out in block letters similar to the ones on the strips of white tape, read as follows:

Viewed from the outermost reaches of space, the earth is no larger than a speck of dust. Remember that the next time you write the word "humanity."

From the look of disgust that comes over his face as he scans these sentences, we can be fairly confident that Mr. Blank has not lost the ability to read. But who the author of these sentences might be is still open to question.

Mr. Blank reaches out for the next page on the pile and discovers that it is a typed manuscript of some sort. The first paragraph reads:

The moment I started to tell my story, they knocked me down and kicked me in the head. When I climbed to my feet and started to talk again, one of them hit me across the mouth, and then another one punched me in the stomach. I fell down. I managed to get up again, but just as I was about to begin the story for the third time, the Colonel threw me against the wall and I passed out.

There are two more paragraphs on the page, but before Mr. Blank can begin reading the second one, the telephone rings. It is a black rotary model from the late forties or early fifties of the past century, and since it is located on the bedside table, Mr. Blank is forced to stand up from the soft leather chair and shuffle over to the other side of the room. He picks up the receiver on the fourth ring.

Hello, says Mr. Blank.

Mr. Blank? asks the voice on the other end.

If you say so.

Are you sure? I can't take any chances.

I'm not sure of anything. If you want to call me Mr. Blank, I'm happy to answer to that name. Who am I talking to?

James.

I don't know any James.

James P. Flood.

Refresh my memory.

I came to visit you yesterday. We spent two hours together.

Ah. The policeman.

Ex-policeman.

Right. The ex-policeman. What can I do for you?

I want to see you again.

Wasn't one conversation enough?

Not really. I know I'm just a minor character in this business, but they said I was allowed to see you twice.

You're telling me I have no choice.

I'm afraid so. But we don't have to talk in the room if you don't want to. We can go out and sit in the park if you'd prefer that.

I don't have anything to wear. I'm standing here dressed in pajamas and slippers.

Look in the closet. You have all the clothes you need.

Ah. The closet. Thank you.

Have you had your breakfast, Mr. Blank?

I don't think so. Am I allowed to eat?

Three meals a day. It's still a bit early, but Anna should be coming around pretty soon.

Anna? Did you say Anna?

She's the person who takes care of you.

I thought she was dead.

Hardly.

Maybe it's a different Anna.

I doubt it. Of all the people involved in this story, she's the only one who's completely on your side.

And the others?

Let's just say there's a lot of resentment, and we'll leave it at that.

◆ ◆ ◆

IT SHOULD BE NOTED that in addition to the camera a microphone is embedded in one of the walls, and every sound Mr. Blank makes is being reproduced and preserved by a highly sensitive digital tape recorder. The least groan or sniffle, the least cough or fleeting flatulence that emerges from his body is therefore an integral part of our account as well. It goes without saying that these aural data also include the words that are variously mumbled, uttered, or shouted by Mr. Blank, as with, for example, the telephone call from James P. Flood recorded above. The conversation ends with Mr. Blank reluctantly giving in to the ex-policeman's demand to pay him a visit sometime that morning. After Mr. Blank hangs up the phone, he sits down on the edge of the narrow bed, assuming a position identical to the one described in the first sentence of this report: palms spread out on his knees, head down, staring at the floor. He ponders whether he should stand up and begin looking for the closet Flood referred to, and if that closet exists, whether he should change out of his pajamas and put on some clothes, assuming there are clothes in the closet—if indeed that closet exists. But Mr. Blank is in no rush to engage in such mundane chores. He wants to go back to the typescript he started reading before he was interrupted by the telephone. He therefore stands up from the bed and takes a first tentative step toward the other side of the room, feeling a sudden rush of dizziness as he does so. He realizes that he will fall down if he remains standing any longer, but rather than return to the bed and sit there until the crisis passes, he puts his right hand against the wall, leans the full brunt of his weight against it, and gradually lowers himself to the floor. Now on his knees, Mr. Blank pitches himself for-

ward and plants his palms on the floor as well. Dizzy or
not, such is his determination to reach the desk that he
crawls there on all fours.

Once he manages to climb into the leather chair, he
rocks back and forth for several moments to steady his
nerves. In spite of his physical efforts, he understands
that he is afraid to go on reading the typescript. Why this
fear should have taken hold of him is something he cannot account for. It's only words, he tells himself, and
since when have words had the power to frighten a man
half to death? It won't do, he mutters in a low, barely audible voice. Then, to reassure himself, he repeats the
same sentence, shouting at the top of his lungs: IT
WON'T DO!

Inexplicably, this sudden burst of sound gives him the
courage to continue. He takes a deep breath, fixes his eyes
on the words in front of him, and reads the following two
paragraphs:

They have kept me in this room ever since. From all I
can gather, it is not a typical cell, and it does not seem to
be part of the military stockade or the territorial house of
detention. It is a small, bare enclosure, measuring
roughly twelve feet by fifteen feet, and because of the
simplicity of its design (dirt floor, thick stone walls), I
suspect that it once served as a storehouse for food supplies, perhaps for sacks of flour and grain. There is a single barred window at the top of the western wall, but it is
too far off the ground for me to get my hands on it. I sleep
on a straw mat in one corner, and two meals are given to
me every day: cold porridge in the morning, tepid soup
and hard bread in the evening. According to my calcula-
tions, I have been here for forty-seven nights. This tally
could be wrong, however. My first days in the cell were
interrupted by numerous beatings, and because I can't remember how many times I lost consciousness—nor how

long the oblivions lasted when I did—it is possible that I lost count somewhere and failed to notice when a particular sun might have risen or another might have set.

The desert begins just outside my window. Each time the wind blows from the west, I can smell the sage and juniper bushes, the minima of those dry distances. I lived out there on my own for close to four months, wandering freely from one place to another, sleeping outdoors in all kinds of weather, and to return from the openness of that country to the narrow confines of this room has not been easy for me. I can bear up to the enforced solitude, to the absence of conversation and human contact, but I long to be in the air and the light again, and I spend my days hungering for something to look at besides these jagged stone walls. Every now and then, soldiers walk below my window. I can hear their boots crunching on the ground, the irregular bursts of their voices, the clatter of carts and horses in the heat of the unattainable day. This is the garrison at Ultima: the westernmost tip of the Confederation, the place that stands at the edge of the known world. We are more than two thousand miles from the capital here, overlooking the unmapped expanses of the Alien Territories. The law says that no one is allowed to go out there. I went because I was ordered to go, and now I have returned to give my report. They will listen to me or they won't listen to me, and then I will be taken outside and shot. I am fairly certain of that now. The important thing is not to delude myself, to resist the temptation of hope. When they finally put me up against the wall and aim their rifles at my body, the only thing I will ask of them is to remove the blindfold. It's not that I have any interest in seeing the men who kill me, but I want to be able to look at the sky again. That is the extent of what I want now. To stand out in the open and look up at the immense blue sky above me, to gaze at the howling infinite one last time.

◆ ◆ ◆

MR. BLANK STOPS READING. His fear has been replaced by confusion, and while he has grasped every word of the text so far, he has no idea what to make of it. Is it an actual report, he wonders, and what is this place called the Confederation, with its garrison at Ultima and its mysterious Alien Territories, and why does the prose sound like something written in the nineteenth century? Mr. Blank is well aware of the fact that his mind is not all it should be, that he is entirely in the dark about where he is and why he is there, but he is reasonably certain that the present moment can be situated sometime in the early twenty-first century and that he lives in a country called the United States of America. This last thought reminds him of the window, or, to be more precise, of the window shade, on which a strip of white tape has been attached bearing the word SHADE. With the soles of his feet pressing against the floor and his arms pressing against the armrests of the leather chair, he swivels right by ninety to a hundred degrees in order to have a look at said window shade—for not only is this chair endowed with the ability to rock back and forth, it can turn in circles as well. This last discovery is so pleasing to Mr. Blank that he momentarily forgets why he wanted to look at the window shade, exulting instead in this hitherto unknown property of the chair. He spins around once, then twice, then three times, and as he does so he remembers sitting in the chair at the barbershop as a young boy and being spun around in a similar fashion by Rocco the barber both before and after his hair was cut. Fortunately, when Mr. Blank comes to rest again, the chair is more or less in the same position as when he started going around in circles, which means that he is once again looking at the window shade, and again, after this enjoyable interlude, Mr. Blank wonders if he shouldn't walk over to the window, pull up the shade, and have a look outside to see where he is. Perhaps he's no longer in America, he says to himself, but in some other country, abducted in the dead of night by secret agents working for a foreign power.

His triple revolution in the chair has left him somewhat dizzy, however, and he hesitates to budge from his spot, fearing a recurrence of the episode that forced him to travel across the room on all fours some minutes ago. What Mr. Blank is still unaware of at this point is that in addition to being able to rock back and forth and turn around in circles, the leather chair is further equipped with a set of four small wheels, which would make it possible for him to journey over to the window shade without having to stand up. Not knowing that other means of propulsion are available to him besides his legs, Mr. Blank therefore stays where he is, sitting in the chair with his back to the desk, looking at the once white but now yellowing window shade, trying to remember his conversation the previous afternoon with the ex-policeman James P. Flood. He casts about in his mind for an image, some hint as to what the man looks like, but rather than conjure forth any clear pictures, his mind is once again overwhelmed by a paralyzing sensation of guilt. Before this fresh bout of torments and terrors can build into a full-blown panic, however, Mr. Blank hears someone rapping on the door, and then the sound of a key entering the lock. Does this mean that Mr. Blank is imprisoned in the room, unable to leave except through the grace and good will of others? Not necessarily. It could be that Mr. Blank has locked the door from within and that the person now trying to enter the room must undo that lock in order to cross the threshold, thus sparing Mr. Blank the trouble of having to stand up and open the door himself.

One way or the other, the door now opens, and in walks a small woman of indeterminate age—anywhere between forty-five and sixty, Mr. Blank thinks, but it is difficult to be certain. Her gray hair is cut short, she is dressed in a pair of dark blue slacks and a light blue cotton blouse, and the first thing she does after entering the room is smile at Mr. Blank. This smile, which seems to combine both tenderness and affection, banishes his fears and puts him in a state of calm equilibrium. He has no idea who she is, but he is nevertheless happy to see her.

Did you sleep well? the woman asks.

I'm not sure, Mr. Blank replies. To be perfectly honest, I can't remember if I slept or not.

That's good. It means the treatment is working.

Rather than comment on this enigmatic pronouncement, Mr. Blank studies the woman for several moments in silence, then asks: Forgive me for being such a fool, but your name wouldn't be Anna, would it?

Once again, the woman gives him a tender and affectionate smile. I'm glad you remembered it, she says. Yesterday, it kept slipping out of your mind.

Suddenly perplexed and agitated, Mr. Blank swivels around in the leather chair until he is facing the desk, then removes the portrait of the young woman from the pile of black-and-white photographs. Before he can turn around again to look at the woman, whose name appears to be Anna, she is standing beside him with her hand poised gently on his right shoulder, looking down at the picture as well.

If your name is Anna, Mr. Blank says, his voice quivering with emotion, then who is this? Her name is Anna, too, isn't it?

Yes, the woman says, studying the portrait closely, as if remembering something with equal but opposite feelings of revulsion and nostalgia. This is Anna. And I'm Anna, too. This is a picture of me.

But, Mr. Blank stammers, but . . . the girl in the picture is young. And you . . . you have gray hair.

Time, Mr. Blank, Anna says. You understand the meaning of time, don't you? This is me thirty-five years ago.

Before Mr. Blank has a chance to respond, Anna puts the portrait of her younger self back on the pile of photographs.

Your breakfast is getting cold, she says, and without another word she leaves the room, only to return a moment later, wheeling in a stainless steel cart with a platter of food on it, which she positions alongside the bed.

The meal consists of a glass of orange juice, a slice of buttered toast, two poached eggs in a small white bowl, and a pot of Earl Grey tea. In due course, Anna will help Mr. Blank out of the chair and lead him over to the bed, but first she hands him a glass of water and three pills— one green, one white, and one purple.

What's wrong with me? Mr. Blank asks. Am I sick?

No, not at all, Anna says. The pills are part of the treatment.

I don't feel sick. A little tired and dizzy, maybe, but otherwise nothing too terrible. Considering my age, not too terrible at all.

Swallow the pills, Mr. Blank. Then you can eat your breakfast. I'm sure you're very hungry.

But I don't want the pills, Mr. Blank replies, stubbornly holding his ground. If I'm not sick, I'm not going to swallow these wretched pills.

Rather than snap back at Mr. Blank after his rude and aggressive statement, Anna bends over and kisses him on the forehead. Dear Mr. Blank, she says. I know how you feel, but you promised to take the pills every day. That was the bargain. If you don't take the pills, the treatment won't work.

I promised? says Mr. Blank. How do I know you're telling the truth?

Because it's me, Anna, and I would never lie to you. I love you too much for that.

The mention of the word *love* softens Mr. Blank's resolve, and he impulsively decides to back down. All right, he says, I'll take the pills. But only if you kiss me again. Agreed? But it has to be a real kiss this time. On the lips.

Anna smiles, then bends over once more and kisses Mr. Blank squarely on the lips. In that it lasts for a good three seconds, the kiss qualifies as more than just a peck, and even though no tongues are involved, this intimate contact sends a tingle of arousal coursing through Mr. Blank's body. By the time Anna straightens up, he has already begun to swallow the pills.

Now they are sitting beside each other on the edge of the bed. The food cart is in front of them, and as Mr. Blank drinks down his orange juice, takes a bite of his toast and a first sip of the tea, Anna softly rubs his back with her left hand, humming a tune that he is unable to identify but which he knows is familiar to him, or was once familiar to him. Then he begins to attack the poached eggs, piercing one of the yolks with the tip of the spoon and gathering up a modest combination of yellow and white in the hollow of the utensil, but when he tries to lift the spoon toward his mouth, he is bewildered to discover that his hand is shaking. Not just some mild tremor, but a pronounced and convulsive twitching that he is powerless to control. By the time the spoon has traveled six inches from the bowl, the spasm is so extreme that the better part of the yellow-and-white mixture has splattered onto the tray.

Would you like me to feed you? Anna asks.

What's wrong with me?

It's nothing to worry about, she answers, patting his back in an attempt to reassure him. A natural reaction to the pills. It will pass in a few minutes.

That's some treatment you've cooked up for me, Mr. Blank mutters in a self-pitying, sullen tone of voice.

It's all for the best, Anna says. And it's not going to last forever. Believe me.

So Mr. Blank allows Anna to feed him, and as she calmly goes about the business of scooping out portions of the poached eggs, holding the teacup to his lips, and wiping his mouth with a paper napkin, Mr. Blank begins to think that Anna is not a woman so much as an angel, or, if you will, an angel in the form of a woman.

Why are you so kind to me? he asks.

Because I love you, Anna says. It's that simple.

Now that the meal is finished, the time has come for excretions, ablutions, and the putting on of clothes. Anna pushes the cart away from the bed and then extends her hand to Mr. Blank to help him to his feet. To his immense astonishment, he finds himself standing in front of a door, a door that until now has escaped his notice, and attached to the surface of this door is yet another strip of white tape, marked with the word BATHROOM. Mr. Blank wonders how he could have missed it, since it is no more than a few steps from the bed, but, as the reader has already learned, his thoughts have largely been elsewhere, lost in a fogland of ghostlike beings and broken memories as he searches for an answer to the question that haunts him.

Do you have to go? Anna asks.

Go? he replies. Go where?

To the bathroom. Do you need to use the toilet?

Ah. The toilet. Yes. Now that you mention it, I think that would be a good idea.

Do you want me to help you, or can you manage on your own?

I'm not sure. Let me give it a try, and we'll see what happens.

Anna turns the white porcelain knob for him, and the door opens. As Mr. Blank shuffles into the white, windowless room with the black-and-white tile floor, Anna shuts the door behind him, and for several moments Mr. Blank just stands there, looking at the white toilet against the far wall, suddenly feeling bereft, aching to be with Anna again. Finally, he whispers to himself: Get a grip, old man. You're acting like a child. Nevertheless, even as he shuffles over to the toilet and begins lowering his pajama bottoms, he feels an overpowering urge to cry.

The pajama bottoms fall to his ankles; he sits down on the toilet seat; his bladder and bowels prepare to evacuate their pent-up liquids and solids. Urine flows from his penis, first one stool and then a second stool slide from his anus, and so good does it feel to be relieving himself in this manner that he forgets the sorrow that took hold of him just moments before. Of course he can manage on his own, he tells himself. He's been doing it ever since he was a little boy, and when it comes to pissing and shitting, he's as capable as any person in the world. Not only that, but he's an expert at wiping his ass as well.

Let Mr. Blank have his little moment of hubris, for successful as he is in completing the first part of the operation, the second part does not go nearly as well. He has no trouble lifting himself off the seat and flushing the toilet, but once he does so he realizes that his pajama bottoms are still gathered around his ankles and in order to pull them up he must either bend over or crouch down and grab hold of the waist with his hands. Neither bending nor crouching is an activity he feels particularly comfortable with today, but of the two he is somewhat more fearful of bending, since he understands the potential for losing his balance once he lowers his head, and he is apprehensive that if he should indeed lose his balance, he might fall to the floor and crack his skull against the black-and-white tiles. He therefore concludes that crouching is the lesser of the two evils, although he is far from confident that his knees can bear the strain that will be put upon them. We will never know if they can or can't. Alerted by the sound of the flushing toilet, Anna, no doubt assuming that Mr. Blank has finished the job he set out to do, opens the door and enters the bathroom.

One might think that Mr. Blank would be embarrassed to find himself in such a compromising position (standing there with his pants down, his limp penis dangling between his naked, scrawny legs), but such is not the case. Mr. Blank feels no false modesty in front of Anna. If anything, he is more than glad to let her see whatever there is to see, and instead of hastily crouching down to pull up his pajama bottoms, he begins undoing the buttons of his pajama top in order to remove the shirt as well.

I'd like to have my bath now, he says.

A real bath in the tub, she asks, or just a sponge bath?

It doesn't matter. You decide.

Anna looks at her watch and says, Maybe just a sponge bath. It's getting a bit late now, and I still have to dress you and make the bed.

By now, Mr. Blank has removed both the top and the bottoms of his pajamas as well as his slippers. Unperturbed by the sight of the old man's naked body, Anna walks over to the toilet and lowers the seat cover, which she pats a couple of times with the palm of her hand as an invitation for Mr. Blank to sit down. Mr. Blank sits, and Anna then perches herself beside him on the edge of the bathtub, turns on the hot water, and begins soaking a white washcloth under the spigot.

The moment Anna begins touching Mr. Blank's body with the warm, soapy cloth, he falls into a trance of languid submission, luxuriating in the feel of her gentle hands upon him. She starts at the top and works her way slowly downward, washing his ears and behind his ears, the front and back of his neck, has him turn on the toilet seat in order to move the cloth up and down his back, then turn again in order to do the same to his chest, pausing every fifteen seconds or so to douse the cloth under the spigot, alternately adding more soap to it and rinsing the soap out of it, depending on whether she is about to wash a particular part of Mr. Blank's body or remove the soap from an area that has just been cleaned. Mr. Blank shuts his eyes, his head suddenly emptied of the shadow-beings and terrors that have haunted him since the first paragraph of this report. By the time the washcloth has descended to his belly, his penis has begun to alter its shape, growing longer and thicker and becoming partially erect, and Mr. Blank marvels that even at his advanced age his penis continues to act as it always did, never once modifying its behavior since his earliest adolescence. So much has changed for him since then, but not that, not that one thing, and now that Anna has brought the washcloth into direct contact with that part of his body, he can feel it stiffening to full extension, and as she goes on rubbing and stroking it with the warm sudsy water, it is all he can do not to cry out and beg her to finish the job.

We're feeling frisky today, Mr. Blank, Anna says.

I'm afraid so, Mr. Blank whispers, his eyes still shut. I can't help it.

If I were you, I'd feel proud of myself. Not every man your age is still . . . still capable of this.

It has nothing to do with me. The thing has a life of its own.

Suddenly, the cloth moves over to his right leg. Before Mr. Blank can register his disappointment, he feels Anna's bare hand sliding up and down the well-lubricated erection. Her right hand is continuing to wash him with the cloth, but her left hand is now engaged in this other task for him, and even as he succumbs to the practiced ministrations of that left hand, he wonders what he has done to deserve such generous treatment.

He gasps when the semen comes spurting out of him, and it is only then, after the deed has been done, that he opens his eyes and turns to Anna. She is no longer sitting on the edge of the tub but kneeling on the floor in front of him, wiping up the ejaculation with the washcloth. Her head is down, and therefore he cannot see her eyes, but nevertheless he leans forward and touches her left cheek with his right hand. Anna looks up then, and as their eyes meet she gives him another one of her tender and affectionate smiles.

You're so good to me, he says.

I want you to be happy, she answers. This is a hard time for you, and if you can find some moments of pleasure in all this, I'm glad to help.

I've done something terrible to you. I don't know what it is, but something terrible . . . unspeakable . . . beyond forgiveness. And here you are, taking care of me like a saint.

It wasn't your fault. You did what you had to do, and I don't hold it against you.

But you suffered. I made you suffer, didn't I?

Yes, very badly. I almost didn't make it.

What did I do?

You sent me off to a dangerous place, a desperate place, a place of destruction and death.

What was it? Some kind of mission?

I guess you could call it that.

You were young then, weren't you? The girl in the photo.

Yes.

You were very pretty, Anna. You're older now, but I still find you pretty. Just about perfect, if you know what I mean.

You don't have to exaggerate, Mr. Blank.

I'm not. If someone told me that I had to look at you twenty-four hours a day for the rest of my life, I wouldn't have any objections.

Once again, Anna smiles, and once again Mr. Blank touches her left cheek with his right hand.

How long were you in that place? he asks.

A few years. Much longer than I was expecting to be.

But you managed to get out.

Eventually, yes.

I feel so ashamed.

You mustn't. The fact is, Mr. Blank, without you I wouldn't be anyone.

Still . . .

No *still*. You're not like other men. You've sacrificed your life to something bigger than yourself, and whatever you've done or haven't done, it's never been for selfish reasons.

Have you ever been in love, Anna?

Several times.

Are you married?

I was.

Was?

My husband died three years ago.

What was his name?

David. David Zimmer.

What happened?

He had a bad heart.

I'm responsible for that, too, aren't I?

Not really . . . Only indirectly.

I'm so sorry.

Don't be. Without you, I never would have met David in the first place. Believe me, Mr. Blank, it isn't your fault. You do what you have to do, and then things happen. Good things and bad things both. That's the way it is. We might be the ones who suffer, but there's a reason for it, a good reason, and anyone who complains about it doesn't understand what it means to be alive.

IT SHOULD BE NOTED that a second camera and a second tape recorder have been planted in the bathroom ceiling, making it possible for all activities in that space to be recorded as well, and because the word *all* is an absolute term, the transcription of the dialogue between Anna and Mr. Blank can be verified in every one of its details.

The sponge bath goes on for several more minutes, and when Anna has finished washing and rinsing the remaining areas of Mr. Blank's body (legs, front and back; ankles, feet, and toes; arms, hands, and fingers; scrotum, buttocks, and anus), she fetches a black terry-cloth robe from a hook on the door and helps Mr. Blank put it on. Then she picks up the blue-and-yellow striped pajamas and walks into the other room, making sure to leave the door open. While Mr. Blank stands in front of the small mirror above the sink, shaving with a battery-operated electric razor (for obvious reasons, traditional razor blades are forbidden), Anna folds the pajamas, makes the bed, and opens the closet to select Mr. Blank's clothes for the day. She moves quickly and efficiently, as if trying to make up for lost time. So rapid is her completion of these tasks that when Mr. Blank finishes shaving with the electric razor and walks into the other room, he is startled to see that his clothes have already been laid out on the bed. Remembering his conversation with James P. Flood and the mention of the word *closet,* he was hoping to catch Anna in the act of opening the closet door, if indeed the closet exists, in order to determine where it is located. Now, as his eyes scan the room, he sees no sign of it, and another mystery remains unsolved.

He could, of course, ask Anna where it is, but once he sees Anna herself, sitting on the bed and smiling up at him, he is so moved to be in her presence again that the question escapes his mind.

I'm beginning to remember you now, he says. Not everything, but little flashes, bits and pieces here and there. I was very young the first time I saw you, wasn't I?

About twenty-one, I think, Anna says.

But I kept losing you. You'd be there for a few days, and then you'd vanish. A year would go by, two years, four years, and then you'd suddenly pop up again.

You didn't know what to do with me, that's why. It took you a long time to figure it out.

And then I sent you on your . . . your mission. I remember being frightened for you. But you were a real battler back in those days, weren't you?

A tough and feisty girl, Mr. Blank.

Exactly. And that's what gave me hope. If you hadn't been a resourceful person, you never would have made it.

Let me help you with your clothes, Anna says, glancing down at her watch. Time is marching on.

The word *marching* induces Mr. Blank to think about his dizzy spells and earlier difficulties with walking, but now, as he travels the short distance from the threshold of the bathroom to the bed, he is encouraged to note that his brain is clear and that he feels in no danger of falling. With nothing to support the hypothesis, he attributes this improvement to the beneficent Anna, to the mere fact that she has been there with him for the past twenty or thirty minutes, radiating the affection he so desperately longs for.

The clothes turn out to be all white: white cotton trousers, white button-down shirt, white boxer shorts, white nylon socks, and a pair of white tennis shoes.

An odd choice, Mr. Blank says. I'm going to look like the Good Humor man.

It was a special request, Anna replies. From Peter Stillman. Not the father, the son. Peter Stillman, Junior.

Who's he?

You don't remember?

I'm afraid not.

He's another one of your charges. When you sent him out on his mission, he had to dress all in white.

How many people have I sent out?

Hundreds, Mr. Blank. More people than I can count.

All right. Let's get on with it. I don't suppose it makes any difference.

Without further ado, he unties the belt of the robe and lets the robe fall to the floor. Once again, he is standing naked in front of Anna, feeling not the slightest hint of embarrassment or modesty. Glancing down and pointing to his penis, he says: Look how small it is. Mr. Bigshot isn't so big now, is he?

Anna smiles and then pats the bed with the palm of her hand, beckoning him to sit down next to her. As he does so, Mr. Blank is once more thrust back into his early childhood, back to the days of Whitey the rocking horse and their long journeys together through the deserts and mountains of the Far West. He thinks about his mother and how she used to dress him like this in his upstairs bedroom with the morning sun slanting through the venetian blinds, and all at once, realizing that his mother is dead, probably long dead, he wonders if Anna somehow hasn't become a new mother for him, even at his advanced age, for why else would he feel so comfortable with her, he who is generally so shy and self-conscious about his body in front of others?

Anna climbs off the bed and crouches down in front of Mr. Blank. She begins with the socks, slipping one over his left foot and then the other one over his right foot, moves on to the undershorts, which she slides up his legs and, as Mr. Blank stands to accommodate her, farther up to his waist, thus concealing the former Mr. Bigshot, who no doubt will rise again to assert his dominance over Mr. Blank before too many hours have passed.

Mr. Blank sits down on the bed a second time, and the process is repeated with the trousers. When Mr. Blank sits down for the third time, Anna puts the sneakers on his feet, first the left one, then the right one, and immediately begins to tie the laces, first on the left shoe, then on the right shoe. After that, she emerges from her crouch and sits down on the bed beside Mr. Blank to help him with the shirt, first guiding his left arm through the left sleeve, then his right arm through the right sleeve, and finally buttoning the buttons from the bottom up, and all during this slow and laborious procedure, Mr. Blank's thoughts are elsewhere, back in his boyhood room with Whitey and his mother, remembering how she used to do these same things for him with the same loving patience, so many years ago now, in the long-ago beginning of his life.

NOW ANNA IS GONE. The stainless steel cart has vanished, the door has been shut, and once again Mr. Blank is alone in the room. The questions he was meaning to ask her—about the closet, about the typescript concerning the so-called Confederation, about whether the door is locked from the outside or not—have all gone unasked, and therefore Mr. Blank is as much in the dark about what he is doing in this place as he was before Anna's arrival. For the time being, he is sitting on the edge of the narrow bed, palms spread out on his knees, head down, staring at the floor, but soon, as soon as he feels the strength of will to do so, he will stand up from the bed and once more make his way over to the desk to look through the pile of photographs (if he can summon the courage to face those images again) and continue his reading of the typescript about the man trapped in the room in Ultima. For the time being, however, he does nothing more than sit on the bed and pine for Anna, wishing she were still there with him, wishing he could take her in his arms and hold her.

Now he is on his feet again. He tries to shuffle toward the desk, but he forgets that he is no longer wearing his slippers, and the rubber sole of his left tennis shoe sticks on the wood floor—in such an abrupt and unforeseen way that Mr. Blank loses his balance and nearly falls. Damn, he says, damn these stupid little white fucks. He longs to change out of the tennis shoes and put on the slippers again, but the slippers are black, and if he put them on he would no longer be dressed all in white, which was something Anna explicitly asked of him—as per the demand of one Peter Stillman, Junior, whoever on earth he might be.

Mr. Blank therefore abandons the shuffling strides he used with the slippers and travels toward the desk with something that resembles an ordinary walk. Not quite the brisk heel-to-toe step one sees in the young and the vigorous, but a slow and heavy gait whereby Mr. Blank lifts one foot an inch or two off the ground, propels the leg attached to that foot approximately six inches forward, and then plants the entire sole of the shoe on the floor, heel and toe together. A slight pause follows, and then he repeats the process with the other foot. It might not be beautiful to watch, but it is sufficient to his purpose, and before long he finds himself standing in front of the desk.

The chair has been pushed in, which means that in order to sit down, Mr. Blank is obliged to pull it out. In so doing, he finally discovers that the chair is equipped with wheels, for instead of scraping along the floor as he is expecting it will, the chair rolls out smoothly, with scarcely any effort on his part. Mr. Blank sits down, astonished that he could have overlooked this feature of the chair during his earlier visits to the desk. He presses his feet against the floor, gives a little shove, and back he goes, covering a distance of some three or four feet. He considers this an important discovery, for pleasant as rocking back and forth and turning around in circles might be, the fact that the chair can move about the room is potentially of great therapeutic value—as, for example, when his legs are feeling especially tired, or when he is attacked by another one of his dizzy spells. Instead of having to stand up and walk at those times, he will be able to use the chair to travel from place to place in a sitting position, thus conserving his strength for more urgent matters. He feels comforted by this thought, and yet, as he inches the chair back toward the desk, the crushing sense of guilt that largely disappeared during Anna's visit suddenly returns, and by the time he makes it to the desk he understands that the desk itself is responsible for these oppressive thoughts—not the desk as desk, perhaps, but the photographs and papers piled on its surface, which no doubt contain the answer to the question that haunts him. They are the source of his anguish, and even though it would be simple enough to return to the bed and ignore them, he feels compelled to go on with his investigations, tortuous and painful as they might be.

He glances down and notices a pad of paper and a ballpoint pen—objects he does not remember having been there during his last visit to the desk. No matter, he says to himself, and without another thought he picks up the pen with his right hand and opens the pad to the first page with his left. In order not to forget what has happened so far today—for Mr. Blank is nothing if not forgetful—he writes down the following list of names:

> James P. Flood
> Anna
> David Zimmer
> Peter Stillman, Jr.
> Peter Stillman, Sr.

This small task accomplished, he closes the pad, puts down the pen, and pushes them aside. Then, reaching for the top pages on the pile farthest to the left, he discovers that they have been stapled together, perhaps twenty to twenty-five pages in all, and when he puts down the sheaf in front of him, he further discovers that it is the typescript he was reading before Anna's arrival. He assumes that she was the one who stapled the pages together—to make things easier for him—and then, realizing that the typescript is not terribly long, he wonders if he will have time to finish it before James P. Flood comes knocking at the door.

He turns to the fourth paragraph on the second page and begins reading:

For the past forty days, there have been no beatings, and neither the Colonel nor any members of his staff have shown their faces to me. The only person I have seen is the sergeant who delivers my food and changes the slop bucket. I have tried to act in a civil manner with him, always making some small remark when he comes in, but he is apparently under orders to remain silent, and not

once have I extracted a single word from this giant in the
brown uniform. Then, less than an hour ago, an extraordi-
nary event took place. The sergeant unlocked the door,
and in walked two young privates carrying a small
wooden table and a straight-backed chair. They set them
down in the middle of the room, and then the sergeant
came in and put a tall stack of blank paper on the table
along with a bottle of ink and a pen.

—You're allowed to write, he said.

—Is that your way of making conversation, I asked, or
are you trying to give me an order?

—The Colonel says you're allowed to write. You can
take that in any way you choose.

—What if I choose not to write?

—You're free to do what you want, but the Colonel
says it's unlikely that a man in your position would pass
up the opportunity to defend himself in writing.

—I assume he's planning to read what I write.

—It would be logical to assume that, yes.

—Will he be sending it to the capital afterward?

—He didn't speak of his intentions. He simply said
that you were allowed to write.

—How much time do I have?

—The subject wasn't discussed.

—And what if I run out of paper?

—You'll be given as much ink and paper as you need.
The Colonel wanted me to tell you that.

—Thank the Colonel for me, and tell him I understand
what he's doing. He's giving me a chance to lie about what
happened in order to save my neck. That's very sporting
of him. Please tell him that I appreciate the gesture.

—I will convey your message to the Colonel.

—Good. Now leave me in peace. If he wants me to
write, I'll write, but in order to do that, I have to be alone.

I was only guessing, of course. The truth is that I have

no idea why the Colonel did what he did. I would like to think he's begun to pity me, but I doubt it can be as simple as that. Colonel De Vega is hardly a compassionate man, and if he suddenly wants to make my life less uncomfortable, giving me a pen is surely an odd way to go about it. A manuscript of lies would serve him well, but he can't possibly think that I'd be willing to change my story at this late date. He has already tried to make me recant, and if I didn't do it when I was nearly beaten to death, why would I do it now? What it comes down to is a matter of caution, I think, a way of preparing himself for whatever might happen next. Too many people know that I'm here for him to execute me without a trial. On the other hand, a trial is something that must be avoided at all costs—for once the case is taken to court, my story will become public knowledge. By allowing me to put the story in writing, he is gathering evidence, irrefutable evidence that will justify any action he decides to take against me. Assume, for example, that he goes ahead and has me shot without a trial. Once the military command in the capital gets wind of my death, they will be obliged by law to open an official inquiry, but at that point he will only have to give them the pages I've written, and he will be exonerated. No doubt they will reward him with a medal for resolving the dilemma so neatly. It could be that he has already written to them about me, in fact, and that I am holding this pen in my hand now because they instructed him to put it there. Under normal circumstances, it takes about three weeks for a letter to reach the capital from Ultima. If I have been here for a month and a half, then perhaps he received his answer today. Let the traitor put his story in writing, they probably said, and then we'll be free to dispose of him in any way we like.

That is one possibility. It could be that I'm exaggerating my importance, however, and that the Colonel is merely playing with me. Who knows if he hasn't decided to amuse himself with the spectacle of my suffering? Distractions are scarce in a town like Ultima, and unless you're resourceful enough to invent your own, you could easily lose your mind from the boredom. I can imagine the Colonel reading my words out loud to his mistress, the two of them sitting up in bed at night and laughing at my pathetic little phrases. That would be amusing, wouldn't it? Such a welcome diversion, such unholy mirth. If I keep him sufficiently entertained, perhaps he'll let me go on writing forever, and bit by bit I'll be turned into his personal clown, his own jester-scribe scribbling forth my pratfalls in endless streams of ink. And even if he should tire of my stories and have me killed, the manuscript will remain, won't it? That will be his trophy— one more skull to add to his collection.

Still, it is difficult for me to suppress the joy I am feeling at this moment. Whatever Colonel De Vega's motives might have been, whatever traps and humiliations he might have in store for me, I can honestly say that I am happier now than at any time since my arrest. I am sitting at the table, listening to the pen as it scratches along the surface of the paper. I stop. I dip the pen into the inkwell, then watch the black shapes form as I move my hand slowly from left to right. I come to the edge and then return to the other side, and as the shapes thin out, I stop once more and dip the pen into the inkwell. So it goes as I work my way down the page, and each cluster of marks is a word, and each word is a sound in my head, and each time I write another word, I hear the sound of my own voice, even though my lips are silent.

Immediately after the sergeant locked the door, I picked up the table and carried it to the western wall, placing it directly below the window. Then I went back for the chair, put the chair on top of the table, and hoisted myself up—first onto the table, then onto the chair. I wanted to see if I could get my fingers around the bars of the window, hoping I might be able to pull myself up and hang there long enough to catch a glimpse of the outside. No matter how hard I strained, however, the tips of my fingers fell short of the goal. Not wanting to abandon the effort, I removed my shirt and tried flinging it up toward the bars, thinking I might be able to thread it through, then grab hold of the dangling sleeves, and in that way manage to haul myself up. But the shirt wasn't quite long enough, and without a tool of some sort to guide the cloth around the metal posts (a stick, a broom handle, even a twig), I could do no more than wave the shirt back and forth, like a white flag of surrender.

In the end, it is probably just as well to put those dreams behind me. If I can't spend my days looking out the window, then I will be forced to concentrate on the task at hand. The essential thing is to stop worrying about the Colonel, to push all thoughts of him out of my mind and set down the facts as I know them. What he chooses to do with this report is strictly his business, and there is nothing I can do to influence his decision. The only thing I can do is tell the story. Given the story I have to tell, that will be difficult enough.

MR. BLANK PAUSES FOR a moment to rest his eyes, to run his fingers through his hair, to ponder the meaning of the words he has just read. When he thinks about the narrator's failed attempt to climb up and look out the window, he suddenly remembers his own window, or, more precisely, the window shade that covers the window, and now that he has a means of traveling over there without having to stand up, he decides that this is the moment to lift the shade and have a peek outdoors. If he can take stock of his surroundings, perhaps some memory will come back to him to help explain what he is doing in this room; perhaps the mere glimpse of a tree or the cornice of a building or a random patch of sky will furnish him with an insight into his predicament. He therefore temporarily abandons his reading of the typescript to journey toward the wall in which the window is located. When he reaches his destination, he thrusts out his right hand, takes hold of the bottom of the shade, and gives it a quick tug, hoping to engage the spring that will send the shade flying upward. It is an old shade, however, and much of its bounce has been lost, and rather than ascend to reveal the window behind it, it sags down several inches below the sill. Frustrated by this botched attempt, Mr. Blank tugs harder and longer the second time, and just like that, the shade decides to act like a proper shade and goes rolling up to the top of the window.

Imagine Mr. Blank's disappointment when he peers through the window and sees that the shutters have been closed, blocking any possibility of looking out to discover where he is. Nor are these the classic wooden shutters with movable slats that allow a bit of light to filter through; they are industrial-strength metal panels with no apertures of any kind, painted a dull shade of gray, with areas of rust showing through that have begun to corrode the surface. Once Mr. Blank rebounds from his shock, he understands that the situation is not as dire as he supposed. The shutters lock from within, and in order to get his fingers on the lock, all he has to do is raise the window sash to its maximum height. Then, once the latch has been unhooked, he will be able to push the shutters open and look out at the world around him. He knows that he will have to stand up from the chair to gain the leverage necessary for such an operation, but that is a small price to pay, and so he lifts his body out of the seat, checks to make sure the window is unlocked (it is), places the heels of his two hands firmly under the top bar of the sash, pauses for a moment to prepare for the exertions ahead, and then pushes for all he is worth. Unexpectedly, the window does not budge. Mr. Blank stops to catch his breath, then tries again—with the same negative result. He suspects that the window has jammed somehow— either because of excess moisture in the air or an excess of paint that has inadvertently glued the upper and lower halves of the window together—but then, as he examines the top bar of the sash more closely, he discovers something that previously eluded his notice. Two large construction nails, almost invisible because the heads of the nails are painted over, have been hammered into the bar. One large nail to the left, one large nail to the right, and because Mr. Blank knows it will be impossible for him to extract those nails from the wood, the window cannot be opened—not now, he realizes, not later, not ever under any circumstances at all.

Proof has been given at last. Someone, perhaps several someones, has or have locked Mr. Blank in this room and is or are holding him prisoner against his will. At least that is what he concludes from the evidence of the two nails hammered into the window sash, but damning as that evidence might be, there is still the question of the door, and until Mr. Blank determines whether the door is locked from the outside, if indeed it is locked at all, the conclusion he has drawn could well be false. If he were thinking clearly, his next step would be to walk or wheel himself over to the door and investigate the matter at once. But Mr. Blank does not move from his spot by the window, for the simple reason that he is afraid, so afraid of what he might learn from the door that he cannot bring himself to risk a confrontation with the truth. Instead, he sits back down in the chair and decides to break the window. For whether he is locked in or not, he is above all desperate to find out where he is. He thinks about the man in the typescript he has been reading, and then he wonders if he, too, won't eventually be taken outside and shot. Or, even more sinister to his imagination, if he won't be murdered right here in the room, strangled to death by the powerful hands of some thug.

There are no blunt objects in the vicinity. No hammers, for example, no broom handles or shovels, no pickaxes or battering rams, and thus even before he begins, Mr. Blank knows his effort is doomed to defeat. Nevertheless, he gives it a try, for not only is he afraid, he is angry, and in his anger he slips off his right tennis shoe, grips the toe firmly in his right hand, and starts pounding the heel against the glass. A normal window might give way under such an assault, but this is a double-paned thermal window of the strongest quality, and it scarcely trembles as the old man strikes it with his feeble weapon of rubber and canvas. After twenty-one consecutive blows, Mr. Blank gives up and lets the shoe drop to the floor. Now, both angry and frustrated, he pounds his fist against the glass several times, not wanting to let the window have the last word, but flesh and bone are no more effective in cracking the pane than the shoe was. He wonders if smashing his head against the window might not do the trick, but even though his mind is not all it should be, Mr. Blank is still lucid enough to understand the folly of inflicting grave physical harm upon himself in what is no doubt a hopeless cause. With a heavy heart, therefore, he slumps back in the chair and closes his eyes—not only afraid, not only angry, but exhausted as well.

The moment he shuts his eyes, he sees the shadowbeings marching through his head. It is a long, dimly lit procession composed of scores if not hundreds of figures, and among them are included both men and women, both children and old people, and while some are short, others are tall, and while some are round, others are lean, and as Mr. Blank strains to listen in on them, he hears not only the sound of their footsteps but something he would liken to a groan, a barely audible collective groan rising from their midst. Where they are and where they are going he cannot say, but they seem to be tramping through a forgotten pasture somewhere, a no-man's-land of scrawny weeds and barren earth, and because it is so dark, and because each figure is moving forward with his or her head down, Mr. Blank cannot distinguish anyone's face. All he knows is that the mere sight of these figments fills him with dread, and once again he is overwhelmed by an implacable sense of guilt. He speculates that these people are the ones he sent off on various missions over the years, and, as was the case with Anna, perhaps some of them, or many of them, or all of them did not fare so terribly well, even to the point of being subjected to unbearable suffering and/or death.

Mr. Blank can't be sure of anything, but it strikes him as possible that there is a connection between these shadow-beings and the photographs on the desk. What if the pictures represent the same people whose faces he is unable to identify in the scene that is playing itself out in his head? If that is so, then the phantoms he is observing are not figments so much as memories, memories of actual people—for when was the last time anyone took a photograph of a person who did not exist? Mr. Blank knows there is nothing to support his theory, that it is only the wildest of wild conjectures, but there has to be some reason, he tells himself, some cause, some principle to explain what is happening to him, to account for the fact that he is in this room with these photographs and these four piles of manuscripts, and why not investigate a little further to see if there is any truth to this blind stab in the dark?

Forgetting about the two nails hammered into the window, forgetting about the door and whether it is locked from the outside or not, Mr. Blank wheels himself over to the desk, picks up the photographs, and then puts them down directly in front of him. Anna is on top, of course, and he spends a few moments looking at her again, studying her unhappy but beautiful young face, gazing deep into the gaze of her dark, burning eyes. No, he says to himself, we were never married. Her husband was a man named David Zimmer, and now Zimmer is dead.

He puts the photograph of Anna aside and looks at the next one. It is another woman, perhaps in her mid-twenties, with light brown hair and steady, watchful eyes. The bottom half of her body is obscured, since she is standing in the doorway of what looks like a New York apartment with the door only partially open, as if in fact she has just opened it to welcome a visitor, and in spite of the cautious look in her eyes, a small smile is creasing the corners of her mouth. Mr. Blank feels a momentary twinge of recognition, but as he struggles to recall her name, nothing comes to him—not after twenty seconds, not after forty seconds, not after a minute. Given that he found Anna's name so quickly, he assumed he would be able to do it with the others as well. But such, apparently, is not the case.

He looks at another ten pictures with the same disappointing results. An old man in a wheelchair, as thin and delicate as a sparrow, wearing the dark glasses of the blind. A grinning woman with a drink in one hand and a cigarette in the other, wearing a 1920s flapper dress and a cloche hat. A frighteningly obese man with an immense hairless head and a cigar jutting from his mouth. Another young woman, this one Chinese, dressed in a dancer's leotard. A dark-haired man with a waxed mustache, decked out in tails and a top hat. A young man sleeping on the grass in what looks like a public park. An older man, perhaps in his mid-fifties, lying on a sofa with his legs propped up on a pile of pillows. A bearded, scraggly-looking homeless person sitting on a sidewalk with his arms around a large mutt. A chubby black man in his sixties holding up a Warsaw telephone book from 1937–38. A slender young man sitting at a table with five cards in his hand and a stack of poker chips in front of him.

With each successive failure, Mr. Blank grows that much more discouraged, that much more doubtful about his chances with the next one—until, muttering something under his breath in such a low voice that the tape recorder cannot pick up the words, he abandons the effort and pushes the photographs aside.

He rocks back and forth in the chair for close to a minute, doing what he can to regain his mental equilibrium and put the defeat behind him. Then, without giving the matter another thought, he picks up the typescript and begins reading again:

My name is Sigmund Graf. I was born forty-one years ago in the town of Luz, a textile center in the northwestern part of Faux-Lieu Province, and until my arrest by Colonel De Vega, I worked in the demographics division of the Bureau of Internal Affairs. As a young man I earned a bachelor's degree in classical literature from All Souls University and then served as an army intelligence officer in the Southeast Border Wars, taking part in the battle that led to the unification of the Petit-Lieu and Merveil principalities. I was honorably discharged with the rank of captain and received a distinguished service medal for my work in intercepting and decoding enemy messages. On returning to the capital after my demobilization, I entered the Bureau as a field coordinator and researcher. At the time of my departure for the Alien Territories, I had been a member of the staff for twelve years. My last official title was that of Deputy Assistant Director.

Like every citizen of the Confederation, I have known my share of suffering, have lived through prolonged moments of violence and upheaval, and have borne the marks of loss upon my soul. I was not yet fourteen when the riots at the Sanctus Academy in Beauchamp led to the outbreak of the Faux-Lieu Language Wars, and two months after the invasion I saw my mother and younger brother burn to death during the Sacking of Luz. My father and I were among the seven thousand who took part in the exodus to the neighboring province of Neue Welt. The journey covered some six hundred miles and took more than two months to complete, and by the time we reached our destination, our number had been reduced by a third. For the last hundred miles, my father was so weak from illness that I had to carry him on my back, staggering half-blind through the mud and winter rains until we came to the outskirts of Nachtburg. For six months we begged in the streets of that gray city to keep ourselves alive, and when we were finally rescued by a loan from relatives in the north, we were on the point of starvation. Life improved for us after that, but no matter how prosperous my father became in the years that followed, he never fully recovered from those months of hardship. When he died ten summers ago at the age of fifty-six, the toll of his experiences had aged him so much that he looked like a man of seventy.

There have been other pains as well. A year and a half ago, the Bureau sent me on an expedition to the Independent Communities of Tierra Blanca Province. Less than a month after my departure, the cholera epidemic swept through the capital. Many now refer to this plague as the

Blight of History, and considering that it struck just as the long and elaborately planned Unification ceremonies were about to begin, one can understand how it could be interpreted as an evil sign, a judgment on the very nature and purpose of the Confederation itself. I am not personally of that opinion, but my own life was nevertheless permanently altered by the epidemic. Cut off from all news of the city, I went about my work for the next four and a half months, traveling back and forth among the remote, mountainous communities to the south, pursuing my investigations into the various religious sects that had taken root in the area. When I returned in August, the crisis was already over—but not before my wife and fifteen-year-old daughter had disappeared. The majority of our neighbors in the Closterham District had either fled the city or succumbed to the illness themselves, but among those who had remained, not a single person could remember having seen them. The house was untouched, and nowhere in it could I find any evidence to suggest that the disease had infiltrated its walls. I made a thorough search of every room, but no secret was unveiled to me as to how or when they might have abandoned the premises. No missing clothes or jewels, no hastily discarded objects lying about the floor. The house was just as I had left it five months earlier, except that my wife and daughter were no longer in it.

I spent several weeks combing the city for clues of their whereabouts, growing increasingly desperate with each failed attempt to uncover information that would put me on their trail. I began by talking to friends and colleagues, and once I had exhausted the circle of familiars (in which I include my wife's female acquaintances, the parents of my daughter's classmates, as well as the shopkeepers and merchants of our district), I started reaching out to strangers. Armed with portraits of my wife and daughter, I questioned countless doctors, nurses, and volunteers who had worked in the makeshift hospitals and schoolrooms where the sick and dying had been cared for, but among all the hundreds of people who looked at those miniatures, not one could recognize the faces I held in my hand. In the end, there was only one conclusion to be drawn. My darlings had been carried off by the scourge. Along with thousands of other victims, they were lying in one of the mass graves on Viaticum Bluff, the burial ground of the anonymous dead.

I do not mention these things in order to put myself in a sympathetic light. No one has to feel sorry for me, and no one has to make excuses for the errors I committed in the aftermath of these events. I am a man, not an angel, and if the grief that overtook me occasionally blurred my vision and led to certain lapses of conduct, that in no way should cast doubt on the truth of my story. Before anyone tries to discredit me by pointing to those stains on my record, I come forward of my own free will and openly pronounce my guilt to the world. These are treacherous times, and I know how easily perceptions can be twisted by a single word spoken into the wrong ear. Impugn a man's character, and everything that man does is made to seem underhanded, suspect, fraught with double motives. In my own case, the flaws in question stemmed from pain, not malice; confusion, not cunning. I lost my way, and for several months I sought comfort in the obliterating powers of alcohol. Most nights I drank alone, sitting in the darkness of my empty house, but some nights were worse than others. Whenever I encountered one of those bad turns, my thoughts would begin to sabotage me, and before long I would be choking on my own breath. My head would fill with images of my wife and daughter, and again and again I would see their mud-splattered bodies being lowered into the ground, again and again I would see their naked limbs entwined among the limbs of other corpses in the hole, and suddenly the darkness of the house would become too much to bear. I would venture out into public places, hoping to break the spell of those images in the noise and tumult of crowds. I frequented taverns and alehouses, and it was in one of those establishments that I did the most damage to myself and my reputation. The incident occurred on a Friday night in November when a man named Giles McNaughton picked a quarrel with me in the Auberge des Vents. McNaughton claimed that I attacked him first, but eleven witnesses testified otherwise in court, and I was acquitted of all charges. It was no more than a small victory, however, for the fact remained that I had broken the man's arm and shattered his nose, and I never would have responded with such vehemence if I hadn't been going to hell by way of drink. The jury found me innocent, judging that I had acted in legitimate self-defense, but that did not remove the stigma of the trial itself—nor the scandal that broke out when it was discovered that a ranking member of the Bureau of Internal Affairs had been engaged in a bloody barroom brawl. Within hours of the verdict, rumors began circulating that officials from the Bureau had bribed certain members of the jury to vote in my favor. I have no knowledge of any corrupt dealings on my behalf, but I would tend to dismiss those accusations as mere gossip. What I do know for certain is that I had never seen McNaughton before that night. He, on the other hand, knew enough about me to address me by name, and when he approached my table and began to talk about my wife, suggesting that he was privy to information that would help solve the mystery of her disappearance, I told him to go away. The man was after money, and one look at his mottled, unhealthy face convinced me that he was a fraud, an opportunist who had got wind of my tragedy and meant to turn a profit from it. McNaughton apparently didn't like being dismissed in such a perfunctory manner. Instead of excusing himself, he sat down in the chair next to mine and angrily grabbed hold of my vest. Then, pulling me forward until our faces were almost touching, he leaned into me and said, What's the matter, citizen? Are you afraid of the truth? His eyes were full of rage and contempt, and because we were so close to each other, those eyes were the only objects in my field of vision. I could feel the hostility flowing through his body, and an instant later I felt it pass directly into mine. That was when I went after him. Yes, he had touched me first, but the moment I started to fight back, I wanted to hurt him, to hurt him as badly as I could.

That was my crime. Take it for what it was, but don't let it interfere with the reading of this report. Trouble comes to all men, and each man makes his peace with the world in his own way. If the force I used against McNaughton that night was unwarranted, the greater wrong was the pleasure I took in using that force. I do not pardon my actions, but considering my state of mind during that period, it is remarkable that the incident in the Auberge des Vents was the only one in which I did harm to another person. All the other harm was inflicted upon myself, and until I learned to curb my desire for drink (which was in fact a desire for death), I ran the risk of utter annihilation. In the course of time, I managed to take hold of myself again, but I confess that I am no longer the man I used to be. If I have gone on living, it is largely because my work at the Bureau has given me a reason to live. Such is the irony of my predicament. I am accused of being an enemy of the Confederation, and yet for the past nineteen years there has been no servant more loyal to the Confederation than myself. My record shows that, and I am proud to have lived in an age that allowed me to participate in such a vast human endeavor. My work in the field has taught me to love the truth above all else, and therefore I have cleared the air pertaining to my sins and transgressions, but that does not mean I can accept guilt for a crime I did not commit. I believe in what the Confederation stands for, and I have passionately defended it with my words, my deeds, and my blood. If the Confederation has turned against me, it can only mean that the Confederation has turned against itself. I cannot hope for life anymore, but if these pages should fall into the hands of someone with sufficient strength of heart to read them in the spirit with which they were written, then perhaps my murder will not have been an entirely useless act.

FAR OFF IN THE distance, beyond the room, beyond the building in which the room is located, Mr. Blank again hears the faint cry of a bird. Distracted by the sound, he looks up from the page in front of him, temporarily abandoning the dolorous confessions of Sigmund Graf. A sudden feeling of pressure invades his stomach, and before Mr. Blank can decide whether to call that feeling one of pain or simple discomfort, his intestinal tract bugles forth an ample, resonant fart. Ho ho, he says out loud, grunting with pleasure. Hopalong Cassidy rides again! Then he tips back in the chair, closes his eyes, and begins to rock, soon lapsing into one of those dull, trancelike states in which the mind is emptied of all thoughts, all emotions, all connection to the self. Thus trapped in his reptilian stupor, Mr. Blank is, as it were, absent, or at least momentarily cut off from his surroundings, which means that he does not hear the hand that has begun knocking on the door. Worse than that, he does not hear the door open, and therefore, even though someone has entered the room, he is still in the dark as to whether the door is locked from the outside or not. Or soon will be still in the dark, once he emerges from his trance.

Someone taps him on the shoulder, but before Mr. Blank can open his eyes and swivel around in the chair to see who it is, that person has already begun to speak. From the timbre and intonation of the voice, Mr. Blank instantly recognizes that it belongs to a man, but he is perplexed by the fact that it is talking to him in what sounds like a Cockney accent.

I'm sorry, Mr. Blank, the man says to him. I knocked and knocked, and when you didn't open the door, I thought I should come in and see if anything was wrong.

Mr. Blank now swivels around in the chair and takes a close look at his visitor. The man appears to be in his early fifties, with neatly combed hair and a small brown mustache with flecks of gray in it. Neither short nor tall, Mr. Blank says to himself, but more on the short side than the tall, and from his erect, almost ramrod posture as he stands there in his tweed suit, he looks like a military man of some kind, or perhaps a lower-level civil servant.

And you are? Mr. Blank asks.

Flood, sir. First name James. Middle name Patrick. James P. Flood. Don't you remember me?

Dimly, only dimly.

The ex-policeman.

Ah. Flood, the ex-policeman. You were going to pay me a visit, weren't you?

Yes, sir. Exactly, sir. That's why I'm here. I'm paying you the visit now.

Mr. Blank casts his eyes about the room, looking for a chair so he can offer Flood a place to sit, but apparently the only chair in the room is the one he now occupies himself.

Something wrong? Flood asks.

No, no, Mr. Blank replies. I'm just looking for another chair, that's all.

I can always sit on the bed, Flood answers, gesturing to the bed. Or, if you're feeling up to it, we could go to the park across the way. No shortage of benches there.

Mr. Blank points down at his right foot and says: I'm missing a shoe. I can't go outside with only one shoe.

Flood turns around and immediately spots the white tennis shoe on the floor below the window. There's the other one, sir. We could get it back on you in two shakes of a cat.

A cat? What are you talking about?

Just an expression, Mr. Blank. No harm intended. Flood pauses for a moment, looks back at the shoe on the floor, and then says: Well, what about it? Should we put it on or not?

Mr. Blank lets out a long, weary sigh. No, he says, with a tinge of sarcasm in his voice, I don't want to put it on. I'm sick of these goddamned shoes. If anything, I'd rather take the other one off, too.

The moment these words escape his mouth, Mr. Blank is heartened to realize that such an act falls within the realm of possibility, that in this one trifling instance he can take matters into his own hands. Without a moment's hesitation, he therefore bends down and removes the sneaker from his left foot.

Ah, that's better, he says, lifting his legs and wiggling his toes in the air. Much better. And I'm still dressed all in white, aren't I?

Of course you are, Flood says. What's so important about that?

Never mind, says Mr. Blank, waving off Flood's question as of no account. Just sit down on the bed and tell me what you want, Mr. Flood.

The former inspector from Scotland Yard lowers himself onto the foot of the mattress, positioning his body in the left-hand quadrant in order to align his face with the face of the old man, who is sitting in the chair with his back to the desk, roughly six feet away. Flood clears his throat, as if searching for the appropriate words to start with, and then, in a low voice trembling with anxiety, he says: It's about the dream, sir.

The dream? Mr. Blank asks, confounded by Flood's statement. What dream?

My dream, Mr. Blank. The one you mentioned in your report on Fanshawe.

Who's Fanshawe?

You don't remember?

No, Mr. Blank declares in a loud, irritable voice. No, I don't remember Fanshawe. I can hardly remember anything. They're pumping me full of pills, and nearly everything is gone now. Most of the time, I don't even know who I am. And if I can't remember myself, how do you expect me to remember this . . . this . . .

Fanshawe.

Fanshawe . . . And who, pray tell, is he?

One of your operatives, sir.

You mean someone I sent out on a mission?

An extremely perilous mission.

Did he survive?

No one is sure. But the prevailing opinion is that he's no longer with us.

Groaning softly to himself, Mr. Blank covers his face with his hands and whispers: Another one of the damned.

Excuse me, Flood interjects, I didn't catch what you said.

Nothing, Mr. Blank replies in a louder voice. I said nothing.

At that point, the conversation stops for several moments. Silence reigns, and in that silence Mr. Blank imagines that he hears the sound of wind, a powerful wind blowing through a stand of trees somewhere near, quite near, but whether that wind is real or not he cannot say. All the while, Flood's eyes remain fixed on the old man's face. When the silence has become unbearable, he at last makes a timid venture to resume the dialogue. Well? he says.

Well what? Mr. Blank replies.

The dream. Can we talk about the dream now?

How can I talk about another man's dream if I don't know what it is?

That's just the problem, Mr. Blank. I have no memory of it myself.

Then I can't do anything for you, can I? If neither one of us knows what happened in your dream, there's nothing to talk about.

It's more complicated than that.

Hardly, Mr. Flood. It's very simple.

That's only because you don't remember writing the report. If you concentrate now, I mean really focus your mind on it, maybe it will come back to you.

I doubt it.

Listen. In the report you wrote on Fanshawe, you mention that he was the author of several unpublished books. One of them was entitled *Neverland*. Unfortunately, except for concluding that certain events in the book were inspired by similar events in Fanshawe's life, you say nothing about the subject, nothing about the plot, nothing about the book at all. Only one brief aside—written in parentheses, I might add—which reads as follows. I quote from memory: *(Montag's house in chapter seven; Flood's dream in chapter thirty)*. The point being, Mr. Blank, that you must have read *Neverland* yourself, and in that you're one of the only people in the world to have done so, I would deeply appreciate it, appreciate it from the very bottom of my miserable heart, if you would make an effort to recall the content of that dream.

From the way you talk about it, *Neverland* must be a novel.

Yes, sir. A work of fiction.

And Fanshawe used you as a character?

Apparently so. There's nothing strange about that. From what I understand, writers do it all the time.

Maybe they do, but I don't see why you should get so worked up about it. The dream never really happened. It's nothing but words on a page—pure invention. Forget about it, Mr. Flood. It's not important.

It's important to me, Mr. Blank. My whole life depends on it. Without that dream, I'm nothing, literally nothing.

The passion with which the normally reserved ex-policeman delivers this last remark—a passion provoked by the sting of a genuine, soul-rending despair—strikes Mr. Blank as nothing short of hilarious, and for the first time since the opening words of this account, he bursts out laughing. As one might expect, Flood takes offense, for no one enjoys having his feelings trampled upon in such a heartless manner, least of all someone as fragile as Flood is at this moment.

I resent that, Mr. Blank, he says. You have no right to laugh at me.

Maybe not, Mr. Blank says, once the spasm in his chest has subsided, but I couldn't help it. You take yourself so damned seriously, Flood. It makes you look ridiculous.

I might be ridiculous, Flood says, with anger rising in his voice, but you, Mr. Blank . . . you're cruel . . . cruel and indifferent to the pain of others. You play with people's lives and take no responsibility for what you've done. I'm not going to sit here and bore you with my troubles, but I blame you for what's happened to me. I most sincerely blame you, and I despise you for it.

Troubles? Mr. Blank says, suddenly softening his tone, doing his best to show some sympathy. What kind of troubles?

The headaches, for one thing. Being forced into early retirement for another. Bankruptcy for yet another. And then there's the business with my wife, or rather my ex-wife, not to speak of my children, who no longer want anything to do with me. My life is in ruins, Mr. Blank. I walk around the world like a ghost, and sometimes I question whether I even exist. Whether I've ever existed at all.

And you think learning about that dream is going to solve all this? It's highly doubtful, you know.

The dream is my only chance. It's like a missing part of me, and until I find it, I'll never really be myself again.

I don't remember Fanshawe. I don't remember reading his novel. I don't remember writing the report. I wish I could help you, Flood, but the treatment they're giving me has turned my brain into a lump of rusty iron.

Try to remember. That's all I ask of you. Try.

As Mr. Blank looks into the eyes of the shattered ex-policeman, he notices that tears have begun to roll down his cheeks. Poor devil, Mr. Blank says to himself. For a moment or two he considers whether to ask Flood to help him locate the closet, for he remembers now that Flood was the one who mentioned it on the phone earlier that morning, but in the end, after weighing the pros and cons of making such a request, he decides against it. Instead he says: Please forgive me, Mr. Flood. I'm sorry I laughed at you.

• • •

NOW FLOOD IS GONE, and once again Mr. Blank is alone in the room. In the aftermath of their disturbing encounter, the old man feels grumpy and out of sorts, wounded by the unjust and belligerent accusations he was subjected to. Still, not wanting to squander any opportunity to increase his knowledge of his present circumstances, he swivels around in the chair until he is facing the desk, then reaches out for the pad and the ballpoint pen. He understands enough at this point to know that unless he writes it down at once, the name will soon fly out of his head, and he doesn't want to run the risk of forgetting it. He therefore opens the pad to the first page, picks up the pen, and adds another entry to his list:

> James P. Flood
> Anna
> David Zimmer
> Peter Stillman, Jr.
> Peter Stillman, Sr.
> Fanshawe

In writing Fanshawe's name, it occurs to him that a second name was mentioned during Flood's visit as well, a name he heard in association with the reference to Flood's dream in chapter thirty of the book, but grapple as he does to recall what it was, he cannot come up with the answer. Something to do with chapter seven, he says to himself, something to do with a house, but the rest is a blank in Mr. Blank's mind. Galled by his own inadequacy, he nevertheless decides to put down something, hoping the name will come back to him at some future moment. The list now reads as follows:

> James P. Flood
> Anna
> David Zimmer
> Peter Stillman, Jr.
> Peter Stillman, Sr.
> Fanshawe
> Man with house

As Mr. Blank puts down the pen, a word begins resounding in his head, and for several moments after that, as the word continues to echo within him, he senses that he is on the brink of a serious breakthrough, a crucial turning point that will help clarify something about what the future has in store for him. The word is *park*. He remembers now that shortly after entering the room, Flood suggested they hold their conversation in *the park across the way*. If nothing else, that would seem to contradict Mr. Blank's previous assertion that he is being held captive, confined to the space in which these four walls surround him, blocked forever from sallying forth into the world. He is somewhat encouraged by this thought, but he also knows that even if he is allowed to visit the park, that does not necessarily prove he is free. Perhaps such visits are possible only under strict supervision, and once Mr. Blank has savored a welcome dose of sunlight and fresh air, he is promptly led back to the room, whereupon he is again held prisoner against his will. He finds it a pity that he did not have the presence of mind to question Flood about the park—in order to determine whether it is a public park, for example, or merely some wooded or grassy area that belongs to the building or institution or asylum

in which he is now living. More important, he realizes for
what must be the umpteenth time in the past several hours
that it all comes down to the nature of the door, and
whether it is locked from the outside or not. He closes his
eyes and strains to recall the sounds he heard after Flood
left the room. Was it the sound of a bolt sliding shut, the
sound of a key turning in a cylinder plug, or simply the
click of a latch? Mr. Blank cannot remember. By the time
the conversation with Flood came to an end, he was so
agitated by that disagreeable little man and his whining
recriminations that he was too distracted to be paying attention to such petty concerns as locks and bolts and
doors.

Mr. Blank wonders if the moment hasn't finally come
to investigate the matter for himself. Afraid though he
might be, would it not be better to learn the truth once and
for all instead of living in a state of perpetual uncertainty? Perhaps, he says to himself. And then again, perhaps not. Before Mr. Blank can decide whether he has the
courage to travel over to the door at last, a new and more
urgent problem suddenly asserts itself—what might most
accurately be called an *urgent urge*. Pressure has once
again begun to build in Mr. Blank's body. Unlike the earlier episode, which was situated in the general area of his
stomach, this one appears in a spot several inches lower,
in the southernmost region of Mr. Blank's belly. From
long experience with such matters, the old man understands that he has to pee. He considers traveling over to
the bathroom in the chair, but knowing that the chair will
not fit through the bathroom doorway, and further knowing that he cannot execute the pee while sitting in the
chair, that a moment will inevitably come when he will
have to stand up (if only to sit down again on the toilet
seat if he is attacked by another rush of dizziness), he decides to make the journey on foot. He therefore rises from

the chair, pleased to note as he does so that his equilibrium is steady, with no signs of the vertigo that plagued him earlier. What Mr. Blank has forgotten, however, is that he is no longer wearing the white tennis shoes, not to speak of no longer wearing the black slippers, and that there is nothing on his feet anymore but the white nylon socks. In that the material of those socks is exceedingly thin, and in that the wooden floor is exceedingly smooth, Mr. Blank discovers after the first step that it is possible to slide his way forward—not with the rasping shuffle of the slippers, but as if he were moving along on ice skates.

A new form of pleasure has become available to him, and after two or three experimental glides between the desk and the bed, he concludes that it is no less enjoyable than rocking back and forth and spinning around in the chair perhaps even more so. The pressure in his bladder is mounting, but Mr. Blank delays his trip to the bathroom in order to prolong his turn on the imaginary ice by a few moments, and as he skates around the room, now lifting one foot into the air, now the other, or else floating along with both feet on the floor, he again returns to the distant past, not as far back as the era of Whitey the rocking horse or the mornings when he would sit in his mother's lap as she dressed him on the bed, but a long while ago just the same: Mr. Blank in his high middle boyhood, roughly ten years old, perhaps eleven, but on no account as advanced as twelve. It's a cold Saturday afternoon in January or February. The pond in the little town where he grew up has frozen over, and there is the young Mr. Blank, who was then referred to as Master Blank, skating hand in hand with his first love, a girl with green eyes and reddish brown hair, long reddish brown hair tousled by the wind, her cheeks red from the cold, her name now forgotten, but beginning with the letter S, Mr. Blank says to himself, he is certain of that, perhaps Susie, he thinks, or

Samantha or Sally or Serena, but no, none of those, and yet no matter, for in that it was the first time he ever held a girl's hand, what he remembers most keenly now is the sensation of having entered a new world, a world in which holding a girl's hand was a good to be desired above all others, and such was his ardor for this young creature whose name began with the letter *S* that once they stopped skating and sat down on a tree stump at the edge of the pond, Master Blank was bold enough to lean forward and kiss her on the lips. For reasons that both baffled and wounded him at the time, Miss S. burst out laughing, turned away her head, and rebuked him with a sentence that has stayed with him ever since—even now, in his present abject circumstances, when all is not right in his head and so many other things have vanished: Don't be silly. For the object of his affections understood nothing of such matters, being but ten or eleven years old and not yet ripened to the point where amorous advances from a member of the opposite sex would have any meaning for her. And so, rather than respond to Master Blank's kiss with a kiss of her own, she laughed.

The rebuff lingered for days afterward, causing such pain in his soul that one morning, noticing her son's grim demeanor, his mother asked him what was wrong. Mr. Blank was still young enough to feel no compunctions about confiding in his mother, and therefore he told her the full story. To which she replied: Don't worry; there are other pebbles on the shore. It was the first time Mr. Blank had heard the expression, and he found it curious that girls should be compared to pebbles, whom they in no way resembled, he felt, at least not in his experience. Nevertheless, he grasped the metaphor, but in spite of understanding what his mother was trying to tell him, he disagreed with her, since passion is and always will be blind to all but one thing, and as far as Mr. Blank was concerned, there was only one pebble on the shore that counted, and if he couldn't have that one, he wasn't interested in any of the others. Time changed all that, of course, and as the years went on he came to see the wisdom of his mother's remark. Now, as he continues to glide around the room in his white nylon socks, he wonders how many pebbles there have been since then. Mr. Blank can't be sure, for his memory is nothing if not defective, but he knows there are dozens, perhaps even scores of them—more pebbles in his past than he can possibly count, right up to and including Anna, the long-lost girl of so many years ago, rediscovered this very day on the infinite shore of love.

These musings fly through Mr. Blank's head in a matter of seconds, perhaps twelve, perhaps twenty, and all the while, as the past wells up within him, he struggles to maintain his concentration so as not to lose his balance as he skates around the room. Short as those seconds may be, however, a moment comes when the bygone days overtake the present, and instead of thinking and moving at the same time, Mr. Blank forgets that he is moving and focuses exclusively on his thoughts, and not long after that, perhaps less than a second, two seconds at most, his feet slip out from under him and he falls to the floor.

Luckily, he does not land on his head, but in all other respects the tumble qualifies as a nasty spill. Pitching backward into the void as his stockinged feet struggle to gain a purchase on the slippery wooden planks, he thrusts his hands out behind him in the vain hope of softening the impact, but he nevertheless hits the floor smack on his tailbone, which sends forth a cascade of volcanic fire through his legs and torso, and given that he has also fallen on his hands, his wrists and elbows are suddenly ablaze as well. Mr. Blank writhes around on the floor, too stunned even to feel sorry for himself, and as he wrestles

to absorb the pain that has engulfed him, he forgets to
contract the muscles in and around his penis, which he
has been doing for the last little while as he skated into
his past. For Mr. Blank's bladder is full to bursting, and
without making a conscious effort to hold it in, as it were,
he is on the verge of producing a shameful and embar-
rassing accident. But the pain is too much for him. It has
pushed all other thoughts out of his mind, and once he begins to relax the aforementioned muscles, he feels his
urethra give way to the inevitable, and a moment later he
is pissing in his pants. No better than an infant, he says to
himself as the warm urine flows out of him and runs down
his leg. Then he adds: Mewling and puking in his nurse's
arms. And then, once the deluge has ceased, he shouts at
the top of his lungs: Idiot! Idiot old man! What the hell is
wrong with you?

NOW MR. BLANK IS in the bathroom, stripping off his pants,
underwear, and socks, all of which have been drenched
and yellowed by his involuntary loss of control. Still rat-
tled by the blunder, his bones still aching from the crash
to the floor, he flings each article of clothing angrily into
the tub, then takes the white washcloth Anna used for the
sponge bath earlier and wipes down his legs and crotch
with warm water. As he does so, his penis begins to swell
from its present flaccid state, rising from the perpendicu-
lar to a forty-five-degree angle. In spite of the multiple in-
dignities Mr. Blank has been subjected to in the past
minutes, he can't help feeling consoled by this develop-
ment, as if it somehow proved that his honor was still intact. After a few more tugs, his old companion is sticking
out from his body at a full ninety-degree thrust, and in
this way, preceded by his second erection of the morning,

Mr. Blank exits the bathroom, walks over to the bed, and climbs into the pajama bottoms that Anna stowed under the pillow. Mr. Bigshot has already begun to shrink by the time the old man pushes his feet into his leather slippers, but what else can be expected in the absence of further friction or mental stimulation of some kind? Mr. Blank feels more comfortable in the pajama bottoms and slippers than he did in the white trousers and tennis shoes, but at the same time he can't help feeling guilty about these sartorial changes, for the fact is that he is no longer dressed all in white, which means that he has broken his promise to Anna—as per the demand of Peter Stillman, Junior—and this pains him deeply, even more deeply than the physical pain that is still reverberating through his body. As he shuffles over to the desk to resume his reading of the typescript, he resolves to make a clean breast of it the next time he sees her, hoping she will find it in her heart to forgive him.

Several moments later, he is once again sitting in the chair, his tailbone throbbing as he wriggles his backside around until he settles into a more or less acceptable position. Then he begins to read:

I first heard about the trouble in the Alien Territories six months ago. It was a late afternoon in midsummer, and I was sitting alone in my office, working on the last pages of my semi-annual report. We were well into the season of white cotton suits by then, but the air that day had been especially hot, bearing down with such stifling heaviness that even the thinnest clothing felt excessive. At ten o'clock, I had instructed the men in my department to remove their coats and ties, but as that seemed to have little effect, I dismissed them at noon. Since the staff had done nothing all morning but fan their faces and wipe sweat from their foreheads, it seemed pointless to hold them hostage any longer.

I remember dining at the Bruder Hof, a small restaurant around the corner from the Foreign Ministry building. Afterward, I took a stroll down Santa Victoria Boulevard, going as far as the river to see if I couldn't coax a breeze to blow against my face. I saw the children launching their toy boats into the water, the women walking by in groups of three and four with their yellow parasols and bashful smiles, the young men loafing on the grass. I have always loved the capital in summer. There is a stillness that envelops us at that time of year, a trance-like quality that seems to blur the difference between animate and inanimate things, and with the crowds along the avenues so much thinner and quieter, the frenzy of the other seasons becomes almost unimaginable. Perhaps it is because the Protector and his family are gone from the city then, and with the palace standing empty and blue shutters covering the familiar windows, the reality of the Confederation begins to feel less substantial. One is aware of the great distances, of the endless territories and people, of the chaos and clamor of lives being lived—but they are all at a remove, somehow, as if the Confederation had become something internal, a dream that each person carried within himself.

After I returned to the office, I worked steadily until four o'clock. I had just put down my pen to mull over the concluding paragraphs when I was interrupted by the arrival of the Minister's secretary—a young man named Jensen or Johnson, I can't recall which. He handed me a note and then looked off discreetly in the other direction while I read it, waiting for an answer to carry back to the Minister. The message was very brief. *Would it be possible for you to stop by my house this evening? Excuse the last-minute invitation, but there is a matter of great importance I need to discuss with you. Joubert.*

I wrote out a reply on department stationery, thanking

the Minister for his invitation and telling him that he
could expect me at eight. The redheaded secretary went
off with the letter, and for the next few minutes I remained at my desk, puzzling over what had just happened. Joubert had been installed as Minister three
months earlier, and in that time I had seen him only
once—at a formal banquet held by the Bureau to celebrate his appointment. Under ordinary circumstances, a
man in my position would have little direct contact with
the Minister, and I found it odd to have been invited to his
house, especially on such short notice. From all I had
heard about him so far, he was neither an impulsive nor
flamboyant administrator, and he did not flaunt his power
in an arbitrary or unreasonable way. I doubted that I had
been summoned to this private meeting because he was
planning to criticize my work, but at the same time, judging from the urgency of his message, it was clear that this
was to be more than just a social visit.

For a person who had attained such an exalted rank,
Joubert did not cut an impressive figure. Just short of his
sixtieth birthday, he was a squat and diminutive man
with bad eyesight and a bulbous nose who continually
adjusted and readjusted his pince-nez throughout our
conversation. A servant led me down the central corridor
to a small library on the ground floor of the Minister's
residence, and when Joubert rose to welcome me,
dressed in an out-of-fashion brown frock coat and a ruf-
fled white cravat, I had the feeling that I was shaking
hands with an assistant law clerk rather than one of the
most important men in the Confederation. Once we began to speak, however, that illusion was quickly dis-
pelled. He had a clear and attentive mind, and each one
of his remarks was delivered with authority and conviction. After he had apologized for calling me to his house
at such an inopportune moment, he gestured to the

gilded leather chair on the opposite side of his desk, and
I sat down.

—I take it you've heard of Ernesto Land, he said, wast-
ing no more time on empty formalities.

—He was one of my closest friends, I replied. We
fought together in the Southeast Border Wars and then
worked as colleagues in the same intelligence division.
After the Consolidation Treaty of the Fourth of March,
he introduced me to the woman I eventually married—
my late wife, Beatrice. A man of exceptional courage and
ability. His death during the cholera epidemic was a great
loss to me.

—That's the official story. A death certificate is on file
at the Municipal Hall of Records, but Land's name has
cropped up again recently on several occasions. If these
reports are true, it would appear he's still alive.

—That's excellent news, sir. It makes me very glad.

—For the past several months, rumors have been drift-
ing back to us from the garrison at Ultima. Nothing has
been confirmed, but according to these stories, Land
crossed over the border into the Alien Territories sometime after the cholera epidemic ended. It's a three-week
journey from the capital to Ultima. That would mean Land
departed just after the outbreak of the scourge. Not dead,
then—simply missing.

—The Alien Territories are off-limits. Everyone
knows that. The No-Entrance Decrees have been in force
for ten years now.

—Nevertheless, Land is there. If the intelligence reports are correct, he was traveling with an army of more
than a hundred men.

—I don't understand.

—We think he's stirring up discontent among the
Primitives, preparing to lead them in an insurrection
against the western provinces.

—That's impossible.

—Nothing is impossible, Graf. You of all people should know that.

—No one believes in the principles of the Confederation more fervently than he does. Ernesto Land is a patriot.

—Men sometimes change their views.

—You must be mistaken. An uprising is impossible. Military action would require unity among the Primitives, and that has never happened and never will. They're as various and divided as we are. Their social customs, their languages, and their religious beliefs have kept them at odds for centuries. The Tackamen in the east bury their dead, just as we do. The Gangi in the west put their dead on elevated platforms and leave the corpses to rot in the sun. The Crow People in the south burn their dead. The Vahntoo in the north cook the bodies and eat them. We call it an offense against God, but to them it's a sacred ritual. Each nation is divided into tribes, which are further subdivided into small clans, and not only have all the nations fought against one another at various times in the past, but tribes within those nations have waged war against one another as well. I simply can't see them banding together, sir. If they were capable of unified action, they never would have been defeated in the first place.

—I understand that you know the Territories quite well.

—I spent more than a year among the Primitives during my early days with the Bureau. That was before the No-Entrance Decrees, of course. I moved from one clan to another, studying the workings of each society, investigating everything from dietary laws to mating rituals. It was a memorable experience. My work since then has always engaged me, but I consider that to have been the most challenging assignment of my career.

—Everything used to be theirs. Then the ships arrived, bringing settlers from Iberia and Gaul, from Albion, Germania, and the Tartar kingdoms, and little by little the Primitives were pushed off their lands. We slaughtered them and enslaved them and then we herded them together in the parched and barren territories beyond the western provinces. You must have encountered much bitterness and resentment during your travels.

—Less than you would think. After four hundred years of conflict, most of the nations were glad to be at peace.

—That was more than ten years ago. Perhaps they've rethought their position by now. If I were in their place, I'd be sorely tempted to reconquer the western provinces. The ground is fertile there. The forests are full of game. It would give them a better, easier life.

—You're forgetting that all the Primitive nations endorsed the No-Entrance Decrees. Now that the fighting has stopped, they would prefer to live in their own separate world, with no interference from the Confederation.

—I hope you're right, Graf, but it's my duty to protect the welfare of the Confederation. Whether they prove groundless or not, the reports about Land must be investigated. You know him, you've spent time in the Territories, and of all the members of the Bureau, I can think of no one better qualified to handle the job. I'm not ordering you to go, but I would be deeply grateful if you accepted. The future of the Confederation could depend on it.

—I feel honored by your confidence in me, sir. But what if I'm not allowed to cross the border?

—You'll be carrying a personal letter from me to Colonel De Vega, the officer in charge of the garrison. He won't be pleased about it, but he'll have no choice. An order from the central government must be obeyed.

—But if what you say is true, and Land is in the Alien Territories with a hundred men, it raises a perplexing question, doesn't it?

—A question?

—How did he manage to get there? From what I'm told, there are troops stationed along the entire frontier. I can imagine one man slipping past them, but not a hundred men. If Land got through, then he must have done it with Colonel De Vega's knowledge.

—Possibly. Possibly not. That's one of the mysteries you'll be entrusted to solve.

—When do you want me to leave?

—As soon as you can. A carriage from the Ministry will be at your disposal. We'll furnish you with supplies and make all the necessary arrangements. The only things you'll need to carry with you are the letter and the clothes on your back.

—Tomorrow morning, then. I've just finished writing my semi-annual report, and my desk is clear.

—Come to the Ministry at nine o'clock for the letter. I'll be waiting for you in my office.

—Very good, sir. Tomorrow morning at nine.

THE MOMENT HE COMES to the end of the conversation between Graf and Joubert, the telephone starts to ring, and once again Mr. Blank is forced to interrupt his reading of the typescript. Cursing under his breath as he extricates himself from the chair, he hobbles slowly across the room toward the bedside table, moving with difficulty because of his recent injuries, and so plodding is his progress that he doesn't pick up the receiver until the seventh ring, whereas he was nimble enough to answer the previous call from Flood on the fourth.

What do you want? Mr. Blank says harshly, as he sits down on the bed, suddenly feeling a flutter of the old dizziness whirling around inside him.

I want to know if you've finished the story, a man's voice calmly answers.

Story? What story is that?

The one you've been reading. The story about the Confederation.

I didn't know it was a story. It sounds more like a report, like something that really happened.

It's make-believe, Mr. Blank. A work of fiction.

Ah. That explains why I've never heard of that place. I know my mind isn't working too well today, but I thought Graf's manuscript must have been found by someone years after he wrote it and then copied out by a typist.

An honest mistake.

A stupid mistake.

Don't worry about it. The only thing I need to know is whether you've finished it or not.

Almost. Just a few more pages to go. If you hadn't interrupted me with this goddamned call, I'd probably be at the end by now.

Good. I'll come round in fifteen or twenty minutes, and we can begin the consultation.

Consultation? What are you talking about?

I'm your doctor, Mr. Blank. I come to see you every day.

I don't remember having a doctor.

Of course not. That's because the treatment is beginning to take effect.

Does my doctor have a name?

Farr. Samuel Farr.

Farr . . . Hmm . . . Yes, Samuel Farr . . . You wouldn't happen to know a woman named Anna, would you?

We'll talk about that later. For now, the only thing you have to do is finish the story.

All right, I'll finish the story. But when you come to my room, how will I know it's you? What if it's someone else pretending to be you?

There's a picture of me on your desk. The twelfth one in from the top of the pile. Take a good look at it, and when I show up, you won't have any trouble recognizing me.

NOW MR. BLANK IS sitting in the chair again, hunched over the desk. Rather than look for Samuel Farr's picture in the pile of photographs as he was instructed to do, he reaches for the pad and ballpoint pen and adds another name to his list:

> James P. Flood
> Anna
> David Zimmer
> Peter Stillman, Jr.
> Peter Stillman, Sr.
> Fanshawe
> Man with house
> Samuel Farr

Pushing aside the pad and pen, he immediately picks up the typescript of the story, forgetting all about his intention to look for Samuel Farr's photograph, in the same way that he has long since forgotten about looking for the closet that is supposedly in the room. The last pages of the text read as follows:

The long journey to Ultima gave me ample time to reflect upon the nature of my mission. A series of coachmen took over the reins at two-hundred-mile intervals, and with nothing for me to do but sit in the carriage and stare out at the landscape, I felt a growing sense of dread as I neared my destination. Ernesto Land had been my comrade and intimate friend, and I had the greatest trouble accepting Joubert's verdict that he had turned traitor to a cause he had defended all his life. He had remained in the military after the Consolidations of Year 31, continuing his work as an intelligence officer under the aegis of the Ministry of War, and whenever he had dined with us at our house or I had met with him for an afternoon meal at one of the taverns near the Ministry Esplanade, he had talked with enthusiasm about the inevitable victory of the Confederation, confident that all we had dreamed of and fought for since our earliest youth would finally come to pass. Now, according to Joubert's agents in Ultima, not only had Land escaped death during the cholera epidemic, he had in fact falsified his death in order to disappear into the wilderness with a small army of anti-Confederationists to foment rebellion among the Primitives. Judging from all I knew about him, this seemed an absurd and preposterous accusation.

Land had grown up in the northwestern farming region of Tierra Vieja Province, the same part of the world where my wife, Beatrice, was born. They had been playmates as small children, and for many years it was taken for granted by their two families that they would eventually marry. Beatrice once confessed to me that Ernesto had been her first love, and when he later turned his back on her and was betrothed to Hortense Chatterton, the daughter of a wealthy shipping family from Mont Sublime, she felt as if her life had ended. But Beatrice was a strong girl, too proud to share her suffering with anyone, and in a demonstration of remarkable courage and dignity, she accompanied her parents and two brothers to the lavish wedding festival at the Chatterton estate. That was where we were introduced. I lost my heart to her that first evening, but it was only after a prolonged courtship of eighteen months that she finally accepted my proposal of marriage. I knew that in her eyes I was no match for Land. I was neither as handsome nor as brilliant as he

was, and it took some time before she understood that
my steadiness of character and fierce devotion to her
were no less important qualities on which to build a life-
long union. Much as I admired Land, I was also aware
of his flaws. There had always been something wild and
obstreperous about him, a headstrong assurance in his
superiority to others, and despite his charm and persua-
siveness, that inborn power to draw attention to himself
wherever he happened to be, one also sensed an incurable
vanity lurking just below the surface. His marriage to
Hortense Chatterton proved to be an unhappy one. He
was unfaithful to her almost from the start, and when she
died in childbirth four years later, he recovered quickly
from his loss. He went through all the rituals of mourning
and public sorrow, but at bottom I felt he was more re-
lieved than brokenhearted. We saw quite a bit of him after
that, much more than had been the case in the early years
of our marriage. To his credit, Land became deeply attached to our little daughter, Marta, always bringing pres-
ents when he visited the house and showering her with
such affection that she came to regard him as a heroic figure, the greatest man who walked the earth. He behaved
with utmost decorum whenever he was among us, and yet
who could fault me if I sometimes questioned whether
the fires that had once burned in my wife's soul for him
had been fully extinguished? Nothing untoward ever
happened—no words or glances between them that could
have aroused my jealousy—but in the aftermath of the
cholera epidemic that had supposedly killed them both,
what was I to make of the fact that Land was now re-
ported to be alive and that in spite of my assiduous efforts to learn something about Beatrice's fate, I hadn't
uncovered a single witness who had seen her in the capital during the scourge? If not for my disastrous run-in
with Giles McNaughton, which had been set off by ugly

innuendos concerning my wife, it seemed doubtful that I
would have tormented myself with such dark suspicions
on my way to Ultima. But what if Beatrice and Marta had
run off with Land while I was traveling through the Independent Communities of Tierra Blanca Province? It
seemed impossible, but as Joubert had said to me the
night before my departure, nothing was impossible, and
of all the people in the world, I was the one who should
know that best.

The wheels of the carriage turned, and by the time I'd
reached the outskirts of Wallingham, the midway point of
the journey, I understood that I was approaching a
twofold horror. If Land had betrayed the Confederation,
my instructions from the minister were to put him under
arrest and transport him back to the capital in chains.
That thought was gruesome enough, but if my friend had
betrayed me by stealing my wife and daughter, then I was
planning to kill him. That much was certain, no matter
what the consequences were. May God damn me for
thinking it, but for Ernesto's sake and my own, I prayed
that Beatrice was already dead.

MR. BLANK TOSSES THE typescript onto the desk, snorting
with dissatisfaction and contempt, furious that he has
been compelled to read a story that has no ending, an unfinished work that has barely even begun, a mere bloody
fragment. What garbage, he says out loud, and then,
swiveling the chair around by a hundred and eighty degrees, he wheels himself over to the bathroom door. He is
thirsty. With no beverages on hand, the only solution is to
pour himself a glass of water from the bathroom sink. He
stands up from the chair, opens the door, and shuffles forward to do just that, all the while regretting having wasted

so much time on that misbegotten excuse of a story. He drinks one glass of water, then another, leaning his left hand on the sink to steady his balance as he gazes forlornly at the soiled clothes in the tub. Now that he happens to be in the bathroom, Mr. Blank wonders if he shouldn't take another shot at peeing, just to play it safe. Worried that he might fall again if he stays on his feet too long, he lets his pajama bottoms drop to his ankles and sits down on the toilet. Just like a woman, he says to himself, suddenly amused by the thought of how different his life would have been if he hadn't been born a man. After his recent accident, his bladder has little to say for itself, but eventually he manages to dribble forth a few measly squirts. He pulls up the pajama bottoms as he climbs to his feet, flushes, rinses his hands at the sink, dries those same hands with a towel, then turns around and opens the door—whereupon he sees a man standing in the room. Another lost opportunity, Mr. Blank says to himself, realizing that the noise of the flushing toilet must have drowned out the sound of the stranger's entrance, thus leaving the question of whether the door is locked from the outside or not unanswered.

Mr. Blank sits down in the chair and does an abrupt half-turn in order to take a look at the new arrival, a tall man in his mid-thirties dressed in blue jeans and a red button-down shirt open at the collar. Dark hair, dark eyes, and a gaunt face that looks as if it hasn't cracked a smile in years. No sooner does Mr. Blank make this observation, however, than the man smiles at him and says: Hello, Mr. Blank. How are you feeling today?

Do I know you? Mr. Blank asks.

Didn't you look at the picture? the man replies.

What picture?

The photograph on your desk. The twelfth one in from the top of the pile. Remember?

Oh, that. Yes. I think so. I was supposed to look at it, wasn't I?

And?

I forgot. I was too busy reading that dumb story.

No problem, the man says, turning around and walking toward the desk, where he picks up the photographs and searches through the pile until he comes to the picture in question. Then, putting the other photographs back on the desk, he walks over to Mr. Blank and hands him the portrait. You see, Mr. Blank? the man says. There I am.

You must be the doctor, then, Mr. Blank says. Samuel . . . Samuel something.

Farr.

That's right. Samuel Farr. I remember now. You have something to do with Anna, don't you?

I did. But that was a long time ago.

Holding the picture firmly in his two hands, Mr. Blank lifts it up until it is directly in front of his face, then studies it for a good twenty seconds. Farr, looking very much as he does now, is sitting in a garden somewhere dressed in a white doctor's coat with a cigarette burning between the second and third fingers of his left hand.

I don't get it, Mr. Blank says, suddenly besieged by a new attack of anguish that burns like a hot coal in his chest and tightens his stomach into the shape of a fist.

What's wrong? Farr asks. It's a good likeness, don't you think?

A perfect likeness. You might be a year or two older now, but the man in the picture is definitely you.

Is that a problem?

It's just that you're so young, Mr. Blank says in a tremulous voice, doing all he can to fight back the tears that are forming in his eyes. Anna is young in her picture, too. But she told me it was taken more than thirty years ago. She's not a girl anymore. Her hair is gray, her husband is dead, and time is turning her into an old woman. But not you, Farr. You were with her. You were in that terrible country I sent her to, but that was more than thirty years ago, and you haven't changed.

Farr hesitates, clearly uncertain about how to answer Mr. Blank. He sits down on the edge of the bed, spreads his palms out on his knees, and looks down at the floor, inadvertently settling into the same position the old man was discovered in at the beginning of this report. A long moment of silence follows. At last he says, speaking in a low voice: I'm not allowed to talk about it.

Mr. Blank looks at him in horror. You're telling me you're dead, he cries out. That's it, isn't it? You didn't make it. Anna lived, but you didn't.

Farr lifts his head and smiles. Do I look dead, Mr. Blank? he asks. We all go through our rough moments, of course, but I'm just as alive as you are, believe me.

Well, who's to say if I'm alive or not? Mr. Blank says, staring grimly at Farr. Maybe I'm dead, too. The way things have been going for me this morning, I wouldn't be a bit surprised. Talk about *the treatment*. It's probably just another word for death.

You don't remember now, Farr says, standing up from the bed and taking the photograph out of Mr. Blank's hands, but the whole thing was your idea. We're just doing what you asked us to do.

Bullshit. I want to see a lawyer. He'll get me out of here. I have my rights, you know.

That can be arranged, Farr answers, carrying the photograph back to the desk, where he reinserts it into the pile. If you like, I'll have someone stop in to see you this afternoon.

Good, Mr. Blank mumbles, somewhat thrown by Farr's solicitous and accommodating manner. That's more like it.

Glancing at his watch, Farr returns from the desk and once again sits down on the bed facing Mr. Blank, who is still in his chair beside the bathroom door. It's getting late, the young man says. We have to begin our talk.

Talk? What kind of talk?

The consultation.

I understand the word, but I have no idea what you mean by it.

We're supposed to discuss the story.

What's the point? It's only the beginning of a story, and where I come from, stories are supposed to have a beginning, a middle, and an end.

I couldn't agree with you more.

Who wrote that piece of drivel, by the way? The bastard should be taken outside and shot.

A man named John Trause. Ever hear of him?

Trause . . . Hmmm . . . Perhaps. He wrote novels, didn't he? It's all a bit fuzzy now, but I think I might have read some of them.

You have. Rest assured that you have.

So why not give me one of those to read—instead of some half-assed, unfinished story without a title?

Trause did finish it. The manuscript comes to a hundred and ten pages, and he wrote it in the early fifties, when he was just starting out as a novelist. You might not think much of it, but it's not bad work for a kid of twenty-three or twenty-four.

I don't understand. Why not let me see the rest of it?

Because it's part of the treatment, Mr. Blank. We didn't put all those papers on the desk just to amuse you. They're here for a purpose.

Such as?

To test your reflexes, for one thing.

My reflexes? What do they have to do with it?

Mental reflexes. Emotional reflexes.

And?

What I want you to do is tell me the rest of the story. Starting at the point where you stopped reading, tell me what you think should happen now, right up to the last paragraph, the last word. You have the beginning. Now I want you to give me the middle and the end.

What is this, some kind of parlor game?

If you like. I prefer to think of it as an exercise in imaginative reasoning.

A pretty phrase, doctor. *Imaginative reasoning.* Since when does the imagination have anything to do with reason?

Since now, Mr. Blank. From the moment you begin to tell me the rest of the story.

All right. It's not as if I have anything better to do, is there?

That's the spirit.

Mr. Blank closes his eyes in order to concentrate on the task at hand, but blocking out the room and his immediate surroundings has the disturbing effect of summoning forth the procession of figment beings who marched through his head at earlier points in the narrative. Mr. Blank shudders at the ghastly vision, and an instant later he opens his eyes again to make it disappear.

What's wrong? Farr asks, with a look of concern on his face.

The damned specters, Mr. Blank says. They're back again.

Specters?

My victims. All the people I've made suffer over the years. They're coming after me now to take their revenge.

Just keep your eyes open, Mr. Blank, and they won't be there anymore. We have to get on with the story.

All right, all right, Mr. Blank says, letting out a long, self-pitying sigh. Give me a minute.

Why don't you tell me some of your thoughts about the Confederation. That might help get you started.

The Confederation . . . The Con-fed-e-ra-tion . . . It's all very simple, isn't it? Just another name for America. Not the United States as we know it, but a country that has evolved in another way, that has another history. But all the trees, all the mountains, and all the prairies of that country stand exactly where they do in ours. The rivers and oceans are identical. Men walk on two legs, see with two eyes, and touch with two hands. They think double thoughts and speak out of both sides of their mouths at once.

Good. Now what happens to Graf when he gets to Ultima?

He goes to see the Colonel with Joubert's letter, but De Vega acts as if he's just been handed a note from a child, since he's in on the plot with Land. Graf reminds him that an order from an official of the central government must be obeyed, but the Colonel says that he works for the Ministry of War, and they've put him under strict orders to abide by the No-Entrance Decrees. Graf mentions the rumors about Land and the hundred soldiers who have entered the Alien Territories, but De Vega pretends to know nothing about it. Graf then says he has no alternative but to write to the Ministry of War and ask for an exemption to bypass the No-Entrance Decrees. Fine, De Vega says, but it takes six weeks for a letter to travel back and forth from the capital, and what are you going to do in the meantime? Take in the sights of Ultima, Graf says, and wait for the response to come—knowing full well that the Colonel will never allow his letter to get through, that it will be intercepted the moment he tries to send it.

Why is De Vega in on the plot? From all I can gather, he appears to be a loyal officer.

He is loyal. And so is Ernesto Land with his hundred troops in the Alien Territories.

I don't follow.

The Confederation is a fragile, newly formed state composed of previously independent colonies and principalities, and in order to hold this tenuous union together, what better way to unite the people than to invent a common enemy and start a war? In this case, they've chosen the Primitives. Land is a double agent who's been sent into the Territories to stir up rebellion among the tribes there. Not so different from what we did to the Indians after the Civil War. Get the natives riled up and then slaughter them.

But how does Graf know that De Vega is in on it, too?

Because he didn't ask enough questions. He should have at least pretended to be curious. And then there's the fact that he and Land both work for the Ministry of War. Joubert and his crowd at the Bureau of Internal Affairs know nothing about the plot, of course, but that's perfectly normal. Government agencies keep secrets from one another all the time.

And then?

Joubert has given Graf the names of three men, spies who work for the Bureau in Ultima. None of them is aware of the others' existence, but collectively they've been the source of Joubert's information about Land. After his conversation with the Colonel, Graf goes out to look for them. But one by one he discovers that all three, as the saying goes, have been dispatched to other parts. Let's find some names for them. It's always more interesting when a character has a name. Captain . . . hmmm . . . Lieutenant Major Jacques Dupin was transferred to a post in the high central mountains two months earlier. Dr. Carlos . . . Woburn . . . left town in June to volunteer his services after an outbreak of smallpox in the north. And Declan Bray, Ultima's most prosperous barber, died from food poisoning in early August.

Whether by accident or design it's impossible to know, but there's poor Graf, completely cut off from the Bureau now, without a single ally or confidant, all alone in that bleak, godforsaken corner of the earth.

Very nice. The names are a good touch, Mr. Blank.

My brain is turning at a hundred miles an hour. Haven't felt so full of beans all day.

Old habits die hard, I suppose.

What's that supposed to mean?

Nothing. Just that you're in good form, beginning to hit your stride. What happens next?

Graf hangs around Ultima for more than a month, trying to figure out a way to cross the border into the Territories. He can't go on foot, after all. He needs a horse, a rifle, provisions, probably a donkey as well. In the meantime, with nothing else to occupy his days, he finds himself getting drawn into Ultima society—such as it is, considering that it's nothing more than a pukey little garrison town in the middle of nowhere. Of all people, it's the hypocrite De Vega who makes a great show of befriending him. He invites Graf to dinner parties—long, tedious affairs attended by military officers, town officials, members of the merchant class, along with their wives, their lady friends, and so on—takes him to the best brothels, and even goes out hunting with him a couple of times. And then there's the Colonel's mistress . . . Carlotta . . . Carlotta Hauptmann . . . a debauched sensualist, the proverbial horny widow, whose principal entertainments in life are fucking and playing cards. The Colonel is married, of course, married with two small children, and since he can visit Carlotta only once or twice a week, she's available for romps with other men. It isn't long before Graf enters into a liaison with her. One night, as they're lying in bed together, he questions her about Land, and Carlotta confirms the rumors. Yes, she says,

Land and his men crossed into the Territories a little more than a year ago. Why does she tell him this? Her motives aren't quite clear. Perhaps she's smitten with Graf and wants to be helpful, or perhaps the Colonel has put her up to it for hidden reasons of his own. This part has to be handled delicately. The reader can never be certain if Carlotta is luring Graf into a trap or if she simply talks too much for her own good. Don't forget that this is Ultima, the dreariest outpost of the Confederation, and sex, gambling, and gossip are about the only fun to be had.

How does Graf make it across the border?

I'm not sure. Probably a bribe of some sort. It doesn't really matter. The important thing is that he gets across one night, and the second part of the story begins. We're in the desert now. Emptiness all around, a ferocious blue sky overhead, pounding light, and then, when the sun goes down, a chill to freeze the marrow in your bones. Graf rides west for several days, mounted on a chestnut horse who goes by the name of Whitey, so called because of a splash of white between the animal's eyes, and since Graf knows the terrain well from his visit twelve years before, he heads in the direction of the Gangi, the tribe with whom he got along best during his earlier travels and whom he found to be the most peaceful of all the Primitive nations. Late one morning, he finally approaches a Gangi encampment, a small village of fifteen or twenty hogans, which would suggest a population of somewhere between seventy and a hundred people. When he's approximately thirty yards from the edge of the settlement, he calls out a greeting in the local Gangi dialect to signal his arrival to the inhabitants—but no one responds. Growing alarmed now, Graf quickens the horse's pace and trots into the heart of the village, where not a single sign of human life can be seen. He dismounts, walks over to one of the hogans, and pushes aside the buffalo skin that serves as the door to the little house. The moment he enters, he's greeted by the overpowering stench of death, the sickening smell of decomposing bodies, and there, in the dim light of the hogan, he sees a dozen slaughtered Gangi—men, women, and children—all of them shot down in cold blood. He staggers out into the air, covering his nose with a handkerchief, and then one by one inspects the other hogans in the village. They're all dead, every last soul is dead, and among them Graf recognizes a number of people he befriended twelve years before. The girls who have since grown into young women, the boys who have since grown into young men, the parents who have since become grandparents, and not a single one is breathing anymore, not a single one will grow a day older for the rest of time.

Who was responsible? Was it Land and his men?

Patience, doctor. A thing like this can't be rushed. We're talking about brutality and death, the murder of the innocent, and Graf is still reeling from the shock of his discovery. He's in no shape to absorb what's happened, but even if he were, why would he think Land had anything to do with it? He's working on the assumption that his old friend is trying to start a rebellion, to form an army of Primitives that will invade the western provinces of the Confederation. An army of dead men can't fight very well, can it? The last thing Graf would conclude is that Land has killed his own future soldiers.

I'm sorry. I won't interrupt anymore.

Interrupt all you like. We're involved in a complicated story here, and not everything is quite what it seems to be. Take Land's troops, for example. They have no idea what their real mission is, no idea that Land is a double agent working for the Ministry of War. They're a bunch of well-educated dreamers, political radicals opposed to the Confederation, and when Land enlisted them to follow him into the Alien Territories, they took him at his word and assumed they were going to help the Primitives annex the western provinces.

Does Graf ever find Land?

He has to. Otherwise, there wouldn't be any story to tell. But that doesn't happen until later, until several weeks or months down the road. About two days after Graf leaves the massacred Gangi village, he comes across one of Land's men, a delirious soldier staggering through the desert with no food, no water, no horse. Graf tries to help him, but it's already too late, and the kid hangs on for just a few more hours. Before he gives up the ghost, he raves on to Graf in a stream of incoherent babble about how everyone is dead, how they never had a chance, how the whole thing was a fraud from the start. Graf has trouble following him. Who does he mean by *everyone*? Land and his troops? The Gangi? Other tribes among the Primitives? The boy doesn't answer, and before the sun goes down that evening, he's dead. Graf buries the body and moves on, and a day or two after that, he comes to another Gangi settlement filled with corpses. He no longer knows what to think. What if Land is responsible, after all? What if the rumor of an insurrection is no more than a blind to cover up a far more sinister undertaking: a quiet slaughter of the Primitives that would enable the government to open their territory to white settlement, to expand the reach of the Confederation all the way to the shores of the western ocean? And yet, how can such a thing be accomplished with such a paucity of troops? One hundred men to wipe out tens of thousands? It doesn't seem possible, and yet if Land has nothing to do with it, then the only other explanation is that the Gangi were killed by another tribe, that the Primitives are at war among themselves.

• • •

MR. BLANK IS ABOUT to continue, but before he can get another word out of his mouth, he and the doctor are interrupted by a knocking at the door. Engrossed as he is in elaborating the story, content as he is to be spinning out his version of far-flung, imaginary events, Mr. Blank instantly understands that this is the moment he's been waiting for: the mystery of the door is about to be solved at last. Once the knock is heard, Farr turns his head in the direction of the sound. Come in, he says, and just like that the door opens, and in walks a woman pushing a stainless steel cart, perhaps the same one Anna used earlier, perhaps one that is identical to it. For once, Mr. Blank has been paying attention, and to the best of his knowledge he heard no sound of a lock being opened—nothing that resembled the sound of a bolt or a latch or a key—which would suggest that the door was unlocked to begin with, unlocked all along. Or so Mr. Blank surmises, beginning to rejoice at the thought of his liberty to come and go as he wants, but a moment later he understands that things are possibly not quite as simple as that. It could be that Dr. Farr forgot to lock the door when he entered. Or, even more likely, that he didn't bother to lock it, knowing he would have no trouble overpowering Mr. Blank if his prisoner tried to escape. Yes, the old man says to himself, that's probably the answer. And he, who is nothing if not pessimistic about his prospects for the future, once again resigns himself to living in a state of constant uncertainty.

Hello, Sam, the woman says. Sorry to barge in on you like this, but it's time for Mr. Blank's lunch.

Hi, Sophie, Farr says, simultaneously looking down at his watch and standing up from the bed. I hadn't realized it was so late.

What's happening? Mr. Blank asks, pounding the arm of his chair and speaking in a petulant tone of voice. I want to go on telling the story.

We've run out of time, Farr says. The consultation is over for today.

But I haven't finished! the old man shouts. I haven't come to the end!

I know, Farr replies, but we're working on a tight schedule around here, and it can't be helped. We'll go on with the story tomorrow.

Tomorrow? Mr. Blank roars, both incredulous and confused. What are you talking about? Tomorrow I won't remember a word I said today. You know that. Even I know that, and I don't know a blasted thing.

Farr walks over to Mr. Blank and pats him on the shoulder, a classic gesture of appeasement for one skilled in the subtle art of bedside manner. All right, he says, I'll see what I can do. I have to get permission first, but if you want me to come back this evening, I can probably work it out. Okay?

Okay, Mr. Blank mumbles, feeling somewhat mollified by the gentleness and concern in Farr's voice.

Well, I'm off then, the doctor announces. See you later.

Without another word, he waves good-bye to Mr. Blank and the woman called Sophie, walks to the door, opens it, steps across the threshold, and shuts the door behind him. Mr. Blank hears the click of the latch, but nothing more. No clatter of a bolt, no turning of a key, and he wonders now if the door isn't simply one of those contraptions that locks automatically the instant you close it.

All the while, the woman called Sophie has been busy wheeling the stainless steel cart alongside the bed and transferring the various dishes of Mr. Blank's lunch from the bottom shelf of the cart to the upper surface. Mr.

Blank notes that there are four dishes in all and that each plate is hidden by a round metal cover with a hole in the center. Seeing those covers, he is suddenly reminded of room-service meals in hotels, which in turn provokes him to speculate on how many nights he has spent in hotels over the course of his life. Too many to count, he hears a voice within him say, a voice that is not his own, at least not a voice he recognizes as his own, and yet because it speaks with such authority and conviction, he acknowledges that it must be telling the truth. If that is the case, he thinks, then he has done a good deal of traveling in his time, moving around from place to place in cars, trains, and airplanes, and yes, he further says to himself, airplanes have taken him all over the world, to many countries on several continents, and no doubt those trips had something to do with the missions he sent all those people on, the poor people who suffered so much because of him, and that is surely why he is confined to this room now, no longer permitted to travel anywhere, stuck inside these four walls because he is being punished for the grave harm he has inflicted on others.

This fleeting reverie is cut off in mid-flow by the sound of the woman's voice. Are you ready for your lunch? she asks, and as he lifts his head to take a look at her, Mr. Blank realizes that he can no longer remember her name. She is somewhere in her late forties or early fifties, and although he finds her face both delicate and attractive, her body is too full and chunky to allow her to be classified as an ideal woman. For the record, it should be noted that her clothes are identical to the ones worn by Anna earlier in the day.

Where's my Anna? Mr. Blank asks. I thought she was the one who takes care of me.

She does, the woman says. But she had some last-minute errands to do, and she asked me to fill in for her.

That's terrible, Mr. Blank says, in a mournful tone of voice. Nothing against you, of course, whoever you might be, but I've been waiting for hours to see her again. That woman is everything to me. I can't live without her.

I know that, the woman says. We all know that. But— and here she gives him a friendly little smile—what can I do about it? I'm afraid you're stuck with me.

Alas, Mr. Blank sighs. I'm sure you mean well, but I'm not going to pretend I'm not disappointed.

You don't have to pretend. You have the right to feel what you feel, Mr. Blank. It's not your fault.

As long as we're stuck with each other, as you put it, I suppose you should tell me who you are.

Sophie.

Ah. That's right. Sophie . . . A very pretty name. And it begins with the letter *S*, doesn't it?

It would seem so.

Think back, Sophie. Are you the little girl I kissed at the pond when I was ten years old? We had just finished ice skating, and then we sat down on a tree stump, and I kissed you. Unfortunately, you didn't kiss me back. You laughed.

It couldn't have been me. When you were ten, I hadn't even been born.

Am I that old?

Not old, exactly. But a lot older than I am.

All right. If you're not that Sophie, which Sophie are you?

Instead of answering him, the Sophie who was not the girl Mr. Blank kissed when he was ten walks over to the desk, retrieves one of the photographs from the pile, and holds it up in the air. That's me, she says. Me as I was about twenty-five years ago.

Come closer, Mr. Blank says. You're too far away.

Several seconds later, Mr. Blank is holding the picture

in his hands. It turns out to be the photograph he lingered over so attentively earlier in the day—the one of the young woman who has just opened the door of what appears to be a New York apartment.

You were much thinner then, he says.

Middle age, Mr. Blank. It tends to do funny things to a girl's figure.

Tell me, Mr. Blank says, tapping the photo with his index finger. What's going on here? Who's the person standing in the hallway, and why do you look like that? Apprehensive, somehow, but at the same time pleased. If not, you wouldn't be smiling.

Sophie crouches down beside Mr. Blank, who is still sitting in the chair, and studies the photo in silence for several moments.

It's my second husband, she says, and I think it's the second time he came to see me. The first time, I was holding my baby in my arms when I opened the door, I remember that distinctly—so this must be the second time.

Why so apprehensive?

Because I wasn't sure how he felt about me.

And the smile?

I'm smiling because I was happy to see him.

Your second husband, you say. And what about the first? Who was he?

A man named Fanshawe.

Fanshawe . . . Fanshawe . . . , Mr. Blank mutters to himself. I think we're finally getting somewhere.

With Sophie still crouching beside him, with the black-and-white photograph of her younger self still on his lap, Mr. Blank abruptly begins to waddle forward in the chair, moving as quickly as he can in the direction of the desk. Once he arrives, he tosses the picture of Sophie on top of Anna's portrait, reaches for the small pad, and opens it to the first page. Running his finger down the list of names, he stops when he comes to *Fanshawe* and then swivels around in the chair to face Sophie, who has climbed to her feet by now and is slowly walking toward him.

Aha, Mr. Blank says, tapping the pad with his finger. I knew it. Fanshawe is implicated in all this, isn't he?

I don't know what you mean, Sophie says, stopping at the foot of the bed and then sitting down in more or less the same spot occupied earlier by James P. Flood. Of course he's implicated. We're all implicated in this, Mr. Blank. I thought you understood that.

Confused by her response, the old man nevertheless struggles to stick to his train of thought. Have you ever heard of someone called Flood? James P. Flood. English fellow. Ex-policeman. Talks with a Cockney accent.

Wouldn't you rather eat your lunch now? Sophie asks. The food is getting cold.

In a minute, Mr. Blank snaps back at her, peeved that she has changed the subject. Just give me a minute. Before we talk about eating, I want you to tell me everything you know about Flood.

I don't know anything. I heard he was around here this morning, but I've never met him.

But your husband . . . your first husband, I mean . . . this Fanshawe . . . He wrote books, didn't he? In one of them, one of them called . . . damn it . . . I can't remember the title. *Never . . . Never-something . . .*

Neverland.

That's it. *Neverland.* He used Flood as one of the characters in that book, and in chapter . . . chapter thirty I think it was, or maybe it was chapter seven, Flood has a dream.

I don't remember, Mr. Blank.

Are you saying that you didn't read your husband's novel?

No, I read it. But it was such a long time ago, and I

haven't looked at it since. You probably won't understand, but for my own peace of mind I've made a conscious decision not to think about Fanshawe and his work.

What ended the marriage? Did he die? Were you divorced?

I married him when I was very young. We lived together for a few years, I got pregnant, and then he vanished.

Did something happen, or did he leave you on purpose?

On purpose.

The man must have been insane. Walking out on a beautiful young thing like you.

Fanshawe was an extremely troubled person. So many good qualities, so many fine things in him, but at bottom he wanted to destroy himself, and in the end he managed to do it. He turned against me, he turned against his work, and then he walked out of his life and disappeared.

His work. You mean he stopped writing?

Yes. He gave up everything. He had great talent, Mr. Blank, but he came to despise that part of himself, and one day he just stopped, he just quit.

It was my fault, wasn't it?

I wouldn't go that far. You played a part in it, of course, but you were only doing what you had to do.

You must hate me.

No, I don't hate you. I went through a tough period for a while, but everything worked out pretty well after that. I got married again, remember, and it's been a good marriage, a long and good marriage. And then there are my two boys, Ben and Paul. They're all grown up now. Ben is a doctor, and Paul's studying to become an anthropologist. Not too bad, if I do say so myself. I hope you get to meet them one day. I think you'll be very proud.

• • •

NOW SOPHIE AND MR. Blank are sitting beside each other on the bed, facing the stainless steel cart with the various dishes of Mr. Blank's lunch lying on the surface, each plate hidden by a round metal cover with a hole in the center. Mr. Blank has worked up an appetite and is eager to begin, but before he is allowed to touch a morsel of food, Sophie tells him, he must first take his afternoon pills. In spite of the understanding that has developed between them over the past several minutes, and in spite of the pleasure Mr. Blank feels at being so close to Sophie's warm and ample body, he balks at this demand and refuses to swallow the medication. Whereas the pills he ingested that morning were green, purple, and white, the ones now sitting on the surface of the stainless steel cart are pink, red, and orange. Sophie explains that they are indeed different pills, designed to produce different effects from the ones he took earlier, and that the treatment will fail unless he takes these in conjunction with the others. Mr. Blank follows the argument, but that in no way convinces him to change his mind, and as Sophie picks up the first pill between her thumb and middle finger and tries to give it to him, Mr. Blank stubbornly shakes his head.

Please, Sophie implores him. I know you're hungry, but one way or another these pills are going into your system before you take a bite of food.

Fuck the food, Mr. Blank says, with bitterness in his voice.

Sophie sighs with exasperation. Look, old-timer, she says, I only want to help you. I'm one of the few people around here who's on your side, but if you won't cooperate, I can think of at least a dozen men who'd be happy to come in here and force these pills down your throat.

All right, Mr. Blank says, beginning to relent somewhat. But only on one condition.

Condition? What are you talking about?

I'll swallow the pills. But first you have to take off your clothes and let me run my hands over your body.

Sophie finds the proposition so ludicrous, she bursts out in a fit of laughter—little realizing that this is exactly how the other Sophie responded under similar circumstances all those many years ago at the frozen pond of Mr. Blank's boyhood. And then, to add insult to injury, she delivers the fatal words: *Don't be silly.*

Ah, says Mr. Blank, tipping backward as if someone has just smacked him across the face. Ah, he groans. Say anything you want, woman. But not that. Please. Not that. Say anything but that.

Within seconds, Mr. Blank's eyes have filled with tears, and before he knows what is happening, the tears are rolling down his cheeks and the old man is crying in earnest.

I'm sorry, Sophie says. I didn't mean to hurt your feelings.

What's wrong with wanting to look at you? Mr. Blank asks, choking through his sobs. You have such beautiful breasts. I just want to see them and touch them. I want to put my hands on your skin, to run my fingers through your pubic hair. What's so terrible about that? I'm not going to hurt you. I just want a little tenderness, that's all. After everything that's been done to me in this place, is that too much to ask?

Well, Sophie says thoughtfully, doubtless feeling some compassion for Mr. Blank's plight, maybe we can come up with a compromise.

Such as? Mr. Blank asks, as he wipes away the tears with the back of his hand.

Such as . . . Such as, you take the pills, and each time you swallow one, I'll let you touch my breasts.

Bare breasts?

No. I'd rather keep my blouse on.

That's not good enough.

All right. I'll take off the blouse. But the bra stays where it is. Understood?

It's not quite paradise, but I suppose I'll have to accept it.

And in that way the matter is resolved. Sophie sheds the blouse, and as she does so Mr. Blank is heartened to see that the bra she is wearing is of the flimsy, lacy variety and not some drab piece of equipment worn by elderly matrons and others who have thrown in the towel on physical love. The upper halves of Sophie's round and abundant breasts are uncovered, and even lower down, the material of the bra is so thin as to allow him a clear view of her nipples jutting against the fabric. Not quite paradise, Mr. Blank says to himself as he downs the first pill with a sip of water, but rather satisfying all the same. And then his hands are upon them—his left hand on the right breast, his right hand on the left breast—and as he savors the bulk and softness of Sophie's somewhat pendulous but noble mammaries, he is further gladdened to observe that she is smiling. Not from pleasure, perhaps, but at least from amusement, thereby demonstrating that she bears him no ill will and is taking the adventure in stride.

You're a dirty old man, Mr. Blank, she says.

I know, he answers. But I was a dirty young man, too.

They work their way through the process twice more—the downing of a pill followed by another delicious encounter with the breasts—and then Sophie puts on her blouse again, and the moment for lunch has arrived.

Unfortunately, the repeated fondling of a desirable woman's flesh has wrought a predictable change in the flesh of the fondler himself. Mr. Blank's old friend is acting up again, and because our hero is no longer wearing the cotton trousers and underpants and is quite naked under the pajama bottoms, there is no barrier to prevent Mr. Bigshot from bounding out through the slit and poking his head into the light of day. This happens at the precise moment Sophie leans forward to begin removing the metal covers from the plates, and as she bends down to store the covers on the lower shelf of the cart, her eyes are just inches from the offending culprit.

Look at you, Sophie says, addressing her words to Mr. Blank's erect penis. Your master squeezes my tits a few times, and now you're all ready for action. Forget it, pal. The fun is over.

I'm sorry, Mr. Blank says, for once truly embarrassed by his behavior. It just kind of popped out on its own. I wasn't expecting it.

No apologies necessary, Sophie replies. Just stick that thing back in your pants, and we'll get down to business.

Business in this case is Mr. Blank's lunch, which consists of a small bowl of now tepid vegetable soup, a club sandwich on white toast, a tomato salad, and a cup of red Jell-O. We will not give an exhaustive account of the consumption of this meal, but one event nevertheless bears mentioning. As was the case after Mr. Blank took his pills in the morning, his hands begin to tremble uncontrollably the instant he tries to eat his food. These might be different pills, designed for different purposes and swathed in different colors, but in the matter of the trembling hands their effect is identical. Mr. Blank begins the meal by attacking the soup. As one might imagine, the inaugural journey of the spoon as it departs from the bowl toward Mr. Blank's mouth is a difficult one, and not a single drop makes it to the intended destination. Through no fault of his own, everything in the spoon comes raining down on Mr. Blank's white shirt.

Good God, he says. I've done it again.

Before the meal can continue, or, more exactly, before the meal can begin, Mr. Blank is obliged to remove the shirt, which is the last article of white clothing he has on, and replace it with the pajama top, thus reverting to the same attire he was discovered in at the beginning of this report. It is a sad moment for Mr. Blank, for now there is not a single trace left of Anna's gentle and meticulous efforts to dress him and prepare him for the day. Even worse, he has now entirely reneged on his promise to wear white.

As Anna did before her, Sophie now takes it upon herself to feed Mr. Blank. Although she is no less kind and patient with him than Anna was, Mr. Blank does not love Sophie in the way he loves Anna, and therefore he looks over her left shoulder at a spot on the far wall as she brings the various spoons and forks to his mouth, pretending it is Anna who is sitting beside him and not Sophie.

Do you know Anna well? he asks.

I met her only a few days ago, Sophie replies, but we've already had three or four long talks. We're very different in all sorts of ways, but we see eye to eye on the stuff that really counts.

Like what?

You, for one thing, Mr. Blank.

Is that why she asked you to fill in for her this afternoon?

I think so.

I've had a pretty awful day so far, but finding her again has done me a lot of good. I don't know what I'd do without her.

She feels the same way about you.

Anna . . . But Anna what? I've spent hours trying to remember her last name. I think it begins with a *B*, but I can't get any further than that.

Blume. Her name is Anna Blume.

Of course! shouts Mr. Blank, striking his forehead with the palm of his left hand. What the hell is wrong with me? I've known that name all my life. Anna Blume. Anna Blume. Anna Blume . . .

NOW SOPHIE IS GONE. The stainless steel cart is gone, the soup-splattered white shirt is gone, the wet and dirty clothes from the tub are gone, and once again, having taken a proper, uneventful pee in the bathroom with Sophie's help, Mr. Blank is alone, sitting on the edge of the narrow bed, palms spread out on his knees, head down, staring at the floor. He ponders the details of Sophie's recent visit, chastising himself for not having asked her any questions about the things that concern him most. Where he is, for example. Whether he is allowed to walk in the park without supervision. Where the closet is, if indeed there is a closet, and why he hasn't been able to find it. Not to mention the eternal enigma of the door—and whether it is locked from the outside or not. Why did he hesitate to bare his soul to her, he wonders, she who is nothing if not a sympathetic person who holds no grudge against him? Is it simply a question of fear, he asks himself, or does it have something to do with the treatment, the noxious, debilitating treatment that has slowly robbed him of the power to stand up for himself and fight his own battles?

Not knowing what to think, Mr. Blank shrugs, slaps his hands on his knees, and rises from the bed. Several seconds later, he is sitting at the desk, the ballpoint pen in his right hand, the little pad in front of him, opened to the first page. He searches the list for Anna's name, discovers it on the second line directly below James P. Flood, and prints out the letters B-l-u-m-e, thus changing the entry from *Anna* to *Anna Blume.* Then, because all the lines on the first page have been filled, he turns to the second page and adds two more entries to the list:

John Trause
Sophie

As he closes the pad, Mr. Blank is dumbfounded to realize that Trause's name returned to him with no effort at all. After so many struggles, so many failures to remember names and faces and events, he considers this to be a triumph of the first magnitude. He rocks back and forth in the chair to celebrate his accomplishment, wondering if the afternoon pills aren't responsible in some way for counteracting his memory loss of the previous hours, or if it isn't just a lucky fluke, one of those unexpected things that happen to us for no apparent reason. Whatever the cause, he decides to go on thinking about the story now, in anticipation of a visit from the doctor that evening, since Farr told him he would do everything possible to allow him to go on telling the story to the end—not tomorrow, when Mr. Blank will no doubt have forgotten the bulk of what he has recounted so far, but today. As the old man goes on tipping back and forth in the chair, however, his eyes fall upon the strip of white tape affixed to the surface of the desk. He has looked at that piece of tape no less than fifty or a hundred times during the course of the day, and each time he did so the white strip was clearly marked with the word DESK. Now, to his astonishment, Mr. Blank sees that it is marked with the word LAMP. His initial response is to think that his eyes have fooled him in some way, so he stops rocking back and forth in order to take a closer look. He leans forward, lowers his head until his nose is nearly touching the tape, and carefully studies the word. To his immense chagrin, he discovers that it still reads LAMP.

With a growing sense of alarm, Mr. Blank clambers out of the chair and begins shuffling around the room, stopping at each strip of white tape attached to an object in order to find out if any other words have been altered. After a thorough investigation, he is horrified to discover that not a single label occupies its former spot. The wall now reads CHAIR. The lamp now reads BATHROOM. The chair now reads DESK. Several possible explanations flare up in Mr. Blank's mind at once. He has suffered a stroke or brain injury of some kind; he has lost the ability to read; someone has played a nasty trick on him. But if he is the victim of a prank, he asks himself, who can be responsible for it? Several people have visited his room in the past few hours: Anna, Flood, Farr, and Sophie. He finds it inconceivable that either one of the women would have done such a thing to him. It's true, however, that his mind was elsewhere when Flood came in, and it's also true that he was in the bathroom flushing the toilet when Farr entered, but he can't imagine how either one of those men could have pulled off such an elaborate switching operation in the short period of time they were not in his field of vision—several seconds at most, scarcely any time at all. Mr. Blank knows that he is not in top form, that his mind is not working as well as it ought to, but he also knows that he is no worse now than he was when the day began, which would dispense with the stroke theory, and if he has lost the ability to read, how could he have made the two recent additions to his list of names? He sits down on the edge of the narrow bed and wonders if he didn't doze off for a few minutes after Sophie left the room. He doesn't remember having fallen asleep, but in the end that is the only explanation that makes sense. A fifth person entered the room, a person who was not Anna or Flood or Farr or Sophie, and switched the labels during Mr. Blank's brief, now forgotten plunge into oblivion.

An enemy is stalking the premises, Mr. Blank says to himself, perhaps several or many of them working in league with one another, and their only intention is to frighten him, to disorient him, to make him think he is losing his mind, as if they were trying to persuade him that the shadow-beings lodged in his head had transformed themselves into living phantoms, bodiless souls conscripted to invade his little room and cause as much havoc as possible. But Mr. Blank is a man of order, and he is offended by the childish mischief-making of his captors. From long experience, he has come to appreciate the importance of precision and clarity in all things, and during the years when he was sending out his charges on their various missions around the world, he always took great pains to write up his reports on their activities in a language that would not betray the truth of what they saw and thought and felt at each step along the way. It will not do, then, to call a chair a desk or a desk a lamp. To indulge in such infantile whimsy is to throw the world into chaos, to make life intolerable for all but the mad. Mr. Blank has not reached the point where he cannot identify objects that do not have their names affixed to them, but there is no question that he is in decline, and he understands that a day might come, perhaps soon, perhaps even tomorrow, when his brain will erode still further and it will become necessary for him to have the name of the thing on the thing in order for him to recognize it. He therefore decides to reverse the damage created by his unseen enemy and return each one of the scrambled labels to its proper spot.

The job takes longer to complete than he thinks it will, for Mr. Blank soon learns that the strips of tape on which the words have been written are endowed with almost supernatural powers of adhesion, and to peel one of them off the surface to which it is attached requires unstinting

concentration and effort. Mr. Blank begins by using his
left thumbnail to pry the first strip loose (the word WALL,
which has landed on the oak board at the foot of the bed),
but no sooner does he manage to slide his nail under the
lower right-hand corner of the tape than the tip of the nail
snaps. He tries again with the nail of his middle finger,
which is somewhat shorter and therefore less frangible,
and diligently hacks away at the stubborn right-hand corner until enough tape has detached itself from the bed for
Mr. Blank to put a small section between his thumb and
middle finger and, tugging gently so as not to cause a tear,
pull the whole strip from the oak board. A satisfying moment, yes, but one that has required a good two minutes
of laborious preparation. Considering that there are
twelve strips of tape to be removed in all, and considering
that Mr. Blank breaks three more fingernails in the process (thus diminishing the number of usable fingers to
six), the reader will understand why it takes him more
than half an hour to finish the job.

These strenuous activities have worn out Mr. Blank,
and instead of pausing to look around the room and ad-
mire his work (which, however small and insignificant it
might appear to be, is for him nothing short of a symbolic
undertaking to restore harmony to a broken universe), he
shuffles off into the bathroom to rinse the sweat from his
face. The old dizziness has returned, and he clutches the
sink with his left hand as he splashes water onto himself
with his right. By the time he turns off the spigot and begins to reach for a towel, he is suddenly feeling worse,
worse than he has felt at any moment of the day so far.
The trouble seems to be located somewhere in his stomach, but before he can pronounce the word *stomach* to
himself, it is traveling up his windpipe, accompanied by
an unpleasant tingling in his jaws. He instinctively
clutches the sink with both hands and lowers his head,

bracing himself against the attack of nausea that has inexplicably overcome him. He fights against it for a second
or two, praying that he can ward off the coming explosion, but it is a hopeless cause, and an instant later he is
vomiting into the sink. They've poisoned me! Mr. Blank
shouts, once the onslaught is over. The monsters have
poisoned me!

WHEN THE ACTION RESUMES, Mr. Blank is stretched out on
the bed, looking up at the white, freshly painted ceiling.
Now that the murderous toxins have been flushed from
his system, he feels drained of energy, half-dead from the
savage bout of puking, retching, and weeping that took
place in the bathroom just minutes ago. And yet, if such a
thing is possible, he also feels better, more tranquil in the
core of his debilitated self, more prepared to face the
trials that no doubt lie ahead.

As Mr. Blank continues to study the ceiling, its white-
ness gradually conjures up an image to him, and instead
of looking at a ceiling he fancies that he is staring at a
sheet of blank paper. Why this should be so he cannot
say, but perhaps it has something to do with the dimen-
sions of the ceiling, which is rectilinear and not square,
meaning that the room is rectilinear and not square as
well, and although the ceiling is much larger than a sheet
of paper, its proportions are roughly similar to those of
the standard eight-and-a-half-by-eleven-inch page. As
Mr. Blank pursues this thought, something stirs inside
him, some distant memory he cannot fix in his mind, that
keeps breaking apart the closer he gets to it, but through
the murk that is blocking him from seeing the thing
clearly in his head, he can dimly make out the contours of
a man, a man who is undoubtedly himself, sitting at a

desk and rolling a sheet of paper into an old manual typewriter. It's probably one of the reports, he says out loud,
speaking in a soft voice, and then Mr. Blank wonders how
many times he must have repeated that gesture, how
many times over the years, understanding now that it was
no less than thousands of times, thousands upon thousands of times, more sheets of paper than a man could
possibly count in a day or a week or a month.

Thinking about the typewriter recalls the typescript he
read earlier in the day, and now that he has more or less
recovered from the exasperating job of peeling off the
strips of white tape and returning them to their correct
spots in the room, and now that the battle that flared up so
violently in his stomach has been quelled, Mr. Blank remembers that he was planning to go on with the story, to
map out the tale to its conclusion in order to prepare himself for the supplementary visit from the doctor that evening. Still stretched out on the bed with his eyes open, he
considers for a moment whether to carry on in silence,
that is, to tell the story to himself in his mind, or else to
continue improvising the events out loud, even if there is
no one in the room to follow what he is saying. Because
he is feeling particularly alone just now, fairly crushed by
the weight of his enforced solitude, he decides to pretend
that the doctor is in the room with him and to proceed as
before, that is, to tell the story with his voice rather than
merely think it in his head.

Let's get on with it, shall we? he says. The Confederation. Sigmund Graf. The Alien Territories. Ernesto Land.
What year is it in this imaginary place? About eighteen-
thirty, I'd guess. No trains, no telegraph. You travel by
horse, and you can wait as long as three weeks for a letter
to arrive. Much like America, but not identical. No black
slaves, for one thing, at least none mentioned in the text.
But more ethnic variety than here for that moment in his-

tory. German names, French names, English names, Spanish names. All right, where were we? Graf is in the Alien Territories, looking for Land, who might or might not be a double agent, who might or might not have absconded with Graf's wife and daughter. Let's back up a little bit. I think I went too fast before, jumped to too many hasty conclusions. According to Joubert, Land is a traitor to the Confederation who's formed his own private army to help lead the Primitives in an invasion of the western provinces. I detest that word, by the way. Primitives. It's too flat, too blunt, has no flair. Let's try to think of something more colorful. Hmmm . . . I don't know . . . Maybe something like . . . the Spirit People. No. No good. The Dolmen. The Olmen. The Tolmen. Awful. What's wrong with me? The Djiin. That's it. The Djiin. Sounds a little like Injun, but with other connotations mixed in as well. All right, the Djiin. Joubert thinks Land is in the Alien Territories to lead the Djiin in an attack on the western provinces. But Graf thinks it's more complicated than that. Why? For one thing, he believes Land is loyal to the Confederation. For another, how could Land have crossed the border accompanied by a hundred men without Colonel De Vega's knowledge? De Vega claims to know nothing about it, but Carlotta has told Graf that Land entered the Territories more than a year ago, and unless she's lying, De Vega is in on the plot. Or else—and this is something I didn't think of before—Land bribed De Vega with a large sum of money, and the Colonel isn't involved at all. But that has nothing to do with Graf, who never suspects the possibility of a bribe. According to his reasoning, Land, De Vega, and the entire military are planning to hatch a phony war with the Djiin in order to hold the Confederation together. Maybe they intend to wipe out the Djiin in the process, maybe not. For the moment, there are only two possibilities: Joubert's position

and Graf's position. If this story is going to add up to anything, though, there has to be a third explanation, something no one ever would have expected. Otherwise, it's
just too damned predictable.

All right, Mr. Blank continues, after a short pause to
focus his thoughts. Graf has come to two Gangi villages,
and the inhabitants of both have been massacred. He's
buried the raving white soldier, and now he doesn't know
what to think. For the time being, as he slowly wends his
way toward Land, let's separate the two main questions
he's confronted with. The professional question and the
private question. What is Land doing in the Territories,
and where are his wife and daughter? To be perfectly
honest, this domestic issue bores me. It can be resolved in
any one of several ways, but each solution is an embarrassment: too trite, too hackneyed, not worth thinking
about. One: Beatrice and Marta have run away with Land.
If Graf finds them together, he's vowed to kill Land. Either he'll succeed or he won't, but at that point the story
devolves into a simple melodrama of a cuckold trying to
defend his honor. Two: Beatrice and Marta have run away
with Land, but Beatrice has died—either from the effects
of the cholera epidemic or from the hardships of living in
the Territories. Assume that Marta, now sixteen, has
grown into a woman and is traveling with Land as his
lover. What does Graf do then? Does he still try to kill
Land, murdering his old friend while his only daughter
begs him to spare the life of the man she loves? Oh
Daddy, please, Daddy, don't do it! Or does Graf let bygones be bygones and forget the whole thing? One way or
the other, it won't wash. Three: Beatrice and Marta have
run away with Land, but both of them have died. Land
won't mention their names to Graf, and that element of
the story turns into a defunct red herring. Trause was apparently quite young when he wrote this piece, and it

doesn't surprise me that he never published it. He worked himself into a corner with the two women. I don't know what solution he came up with, but I'd bet good money that it was the second one—which is just as bad as the first and the third. As far as I'm concerned, I'd just as soon forget about Beatrice and Marta. Let's say they died in the cholera epidemic and leave it at that. Poor Graf, of course, but if you want to tell a good story, you can't show any pity.

Okay, Mr. Blank says, clearing his throat as he tries to pick up the thread of the narrative, where were we? Graf. Graf alone. Graf wandering around the desert on his horse, the good steed Whitey, searching for the elusive Ernesto Land . . .

Mr. Blank stops. A new idea has entered his head, a fiendish, devastating illumination that sends a wave of pleasure shuddering through his body, from the very toes on his feet to the nerve cells in his brain. In a single instant, the whole business has been made clear to him, and as the old man contemplates the shattering consequences of what he now knows is the inevitable choice, the only choice available to him from a horde of contending possibilities, he begins to pound his chest and kick his feet and shake his shoulders as he lets out a whoop of wild, convulsive laughter.

Hold on, Mr. Blank says, raising a hand to his imaginary interlocutor. Scratch everything. I've got it now. Back to the beginning. Part two, that is. Back to the beginning of part two, when Graf slips across the border and enters the Alien Territories. Forget the massacre of the Gangi. Forget the second massacre of the Gangi. Graf steers clear of all Djiin villages and settlements. The No-Entrance Decrees have been in force for ten years, and he knows the Djiin will not take kindly to his presence. A white man traveling alone in the Territories? Impossible.

If they find him, he's as good as dead. So he keeps a wide berth, confining himself to the vast wilderness areas that separate the different nations from one another, looking for Land and his men, yes, encountering the raving soldier, yes, but once he finds what he's looking for, it's altogether the opposite of what he was expecting. On a barren plain in the north-central region of the Territories, a stretch of country similar to the salt flats in Utah, he chances upon a mound of a hundred and fifteen corpses, some of them mutilated, some of them intact, all of them rotting and decomposing in the sun. Not Gangi bodies, not the bodies of any members of the Djiin nations, but white men, white men in soldiers' uniforms, at least those who weren't stripped naked and hacked to pieces, and as Graf stumbles around this putrid, nauseating mass of the slaughtered dead, he discovers that one of the victims is his old friend Ernesto Land—lying on his back with a bullet hole in his forehead and a swarm of flies and maggots crawling over his half-eaten face. We won't dwell on Graf's response to this horror: the puking and weeping, the howling, the rending of his garments. What matters is this. Because his encounter with the raving soldier took place only two weeks earlier, Graf knows the massacre must be fairly recent. But most of all, what matters is this: he has no doubt that Land and his men were murdered by the Djiin.

Mr. Blank pauses to emit another laugh, more restrained than the last one, perhaps, but nevertheless a laugh that manages to express both joy and bitterness at the same time, for even if Mr. Blank is happy to have reshaped the story according to his own design, he knows that it is a gruesome story for all that, and a part of him recoils in terror from what he has yet to tell.

But Graf is wrong, he says. Graf knows nothing about the sinister scheme he's been drawn into. He's the fall guy, as they say in the movies, the patsy who's been set up by the government to put the machinery in motion. They're all in on it—Joubert, the Ministry of War, De Vega, the whole lot of them. Yes, Land was sent into the Territories as a double agent, with instructions to stir up the Djiin into invading the western provinces, which would unleash the war the government so desperately wants. But Land fails in his mission. A year goes by, and when nothing happens after all that time, the men in power conclude that Land has betrayed them, that for one reason or another his conscience has gotten the better of him and he's made peace with the Djiin. So they cook up a new plan and send a second army into the Territories. Not from Ultima, but from another garrison several hundred miles to the north, and this contingent is much larger than the first, at least ten times larger, and with a thousand troops against a hundred, Land and his ragtag bunch of idealists don't have a chance. Yes, you heard me correctly. The Confederation sends in a second army to wipe out the first army. All in secret, of course, and if a man such as Graf should be sent out to look for Land, he would naturally conclude that the Djiin are responsible for that pile of stinking, mutilated corpses. At this point, Graf becomes the key figure in the operation. Without knowing it, he's the person who's going to get the war started. How? By being allowed to write his story in that crummy little cell in Ultima. De Vega works him over in the beginning, beats him constantly for a whole week, but that's only to put the fear of God in him and convince him that he's about to be executed. And when a man thinks he's about to die, he's going to spill his guts on paper the moment he's allowed to write. So Graf does what they want him to do. He tells about his mission to track down Land, and when he comes to the massacre he discovered in the salt flats, he omits nothing, describes the whole abomina-

tion down to the last gory detail. That's the crucial point:
a vivid, eyewitness account of what happened, with all
the blame put on the Djiin. When Graf finishes his story,
De Vega takes possession of the manuscript and releases
him from prison. Graf is stunned. He was expecting to be
shot, and here he is being paid a large bonus for his work
and given a free ride back to the capital in a first-class
carriage. By the time he makes it home, the manuscript
has been skillfully edited and released to every newspa-
per in the country. CONFEDERATION SOLDIERS MASSACRED
BY DJIIN: A Firsthand Report by Sigmund Graf, Deputy
Assistant Director of the Bureau of Internal Affairs.

Graf returns to find the entire population of the capital
up in arms, clamoring for an invasion of the Alien Territories. He understands now how cruelly he's been tricked.
War on this scale could potentially destroy the Confederation, and it turns out that he, and he alone, was the match
that ignited this deadly fire. He goes to Joubert and de-
mands an explanation. Now that things have worked out
so well, Joubert is all too happy to give it to him. Then he
offers Graf a promotion with a large increase in salary,
but Graf counters with an offer of his own: I resign, he
says, and then he marches out of the room, slamming the
door behind him. That evening, in the darkness of his
empty house, he picks up a loaded revolver and fires a
bullet through his skull. And that's it. End of story. *Finità,
la commedia.*

MR. BLANK HAS BEEN talking steadily for nearly twenty
minutes, and he is tired now, and not only from the exertions of his vocal cords, for his throat was irritated to begin with (brought on by the upchuck binge in the
bathroom just minutes before), and he delivers the final

sentences of his tale with a noticeable rasp in his voice.
He closes his eyes, forgetting that such an action is likely
to bring back the procession of figment beings blundering
through the wilderness, the mob of the damned, the face-
less ones who will eventually surround him and tear his
body apart, but this time luck spares Mr. Blank from the
demons, and when he closes his eyes he is once again in
the past, sitting in a wooden chair of some kind, an
Adirondack chair he believes it is called, on a lawn somewhere in the country, some remote and rustic spot he cannot identify, with green grass all around him and bluish
mountains in the distance, and the weather is warm, warm
in the way summer is warm, with a cloudless sky above
and the sun pouring down on his skin, and there is Mr.
Blank, many years ago now it would seem, back in the
days of his early manhood, sitting in the Adirondack
chair and holding a small child in his arms, a one-year-
old girl child dressed in a white T-shirt and a white dia-
per, and Mr. Blank is looking into the eyes of the little girl
and talking to her, what words he cannot say, for this excursion into the past is unfolding in silence, and as Mr.
Blank talks to the little girl, she is looking back at him
with an intent and serious expression in her eyes, and he
wonders now, lying on the bed with his eyes now closed,
if this small person isn't Anna Blume at the beginning of
her life, his beloved Anna Blume, and if it isn't Anna,
whether the child might not be his daughter, but what
daughter, he asks himself, what daughter and what is her
name, and if he is the father of a child, where is the
mother and what is her name, he asks himself, and then
he makes a mental note to inquire about these matters the
next time a person enters the room, to find out if he has a
home somewhere with a wife and children, or once had a
wife, or once had a home, or if this room is not the place
where he has always lived, but Mr. Blank is about to for-

get this mental note and therefore will forget to ask these
questions, for he is extremely tired now, and the image of
himself in the Adirondack chair with the young child in
his arms has just vanished, and Mr. Blank has fallen
asleep.

Because of the camera, which has gone on taking one
picture per second throughout this report, we know for
certain that Mr. Blank's nap lasts for exactly twenty-
seven minutes and twelve seconds. He might have gone
on sleeping much longer than that, but a man has now entered the room, and he is tapping Mr. Blank on the shoulder in an effort to wake him. When the old man opens his
eyes, he feels entirely refreshed by his brief sojourn in the
Land of Nod, and he sits up immediately, alert and ready
for the encounter, with no trace of grogginess clouding
his mind.

The visitor appears to be in his late fifties or early sixties, and like Farr before him, he is dressed in a pair of
blue jeans, but whereas Farr was wearing a red shirt, this
man's shirt is black, and while Farr came into the room
empty-handed, the man in the black shirt is carrying a
thick bundle of files and folders in his arms. His face is
deeply familiar to Mr. Blank, but as with so many of the
faces he has seen today, whether in photographs or in the
flesh, he is at a loss to attach a name to it.

Are you Fogg? he asks. Marco Fogg?

The visitor smiles and shakes his head. No, he says,
I'm afraid not. Why would you think I'm Fogg?

I don't know, but when I woke up just now I suddenly
remembered that Fogg stopped by around this time yesterday. A minor miracle, actually, now that I think about
it. Remembering, I mean. But Fogg came in. I'm certain
of that. For afternoon tea. We played cards for a while.
We talked. And he told me a number of funny jokes.

Jokes? the visitor asks, walking over to the desk,

swiveling the chair by a hundred and eighty degrees, and sitting down with the pile of dossiers on his lap. As he does so, Mr. Blank stands up, shuffles forward for several feet, and then sits down on the bottom edge of the mattress, settling into roughly the same spot that Flood occupied earlier in the day.

Yes, jokes, Mr. Blank continues. I can't remember them all, but there was one that struck me as especially good.

You wouldn't mind telling it to me, would you? the visitor asks. I'm always on the lookout for good jokes.

I can try, Mr. Blank answers, and then he pauses for a few moments to collect his thoughts. Let's see, he says. Hmmm. Let me see. I think it begins like this. A man walks into a bar in Chicago at five o'clock in the afternoon and orders three scotches. Not one after the other, but all three at once. The bartender is a little puzzled by this unusual request, but he doesn't say anything and gives the man what he wants—three scotches, lined up on the bar in a row. The man drinks them down one by one, pays the bill, and leaves. The next day, he comes back at five o'clock and orders the same thing. Three scotches all at once. And the day after that, and every day after that for two weeks. Finally, curiosity gets the better of the barman. I don't mean to be nosy, he says, but you've been in here every day for the past two weeks ordering your three scotches, and I'd just like to know why. Most people take them one at a time. Ah, the man says, the answer is very simple. I have two brothers. One of them lives in New York, one lives in San Francisco, and the three of us are very close. As a way of honoring our friendship, we all go into a bar at five in the afternoon and order three scotches, silently toasting one another's health, pretending that we're all together in the same place. The barman nods, finally understanding the reason for this strange ritual, and thinks no more about it. The business goes on for

another four months. The man comes in every day at five
o'clock, and the bartender serves him the three drinks.
Then something happens. The man shows up at his regu-
lar hour one afternoon, but this time he orders only two
scotches. The bartender is worried, and after a while he
plucks up his courage and says: I don't mean to be nosy,
but every day for the past four and a half months you've
come in here and ordered three scotches. Now you order
two. I know it's none of my business, but I just hope nothing's gone wrong with your family. Nothing's wrong, the
man says, as bright and chipper as ever. What is it, then?
the bartender asks. The answer is very simple, the man
says. I've stopped drinking.

The visitor erupts in a prolonged fit of laughter, and
while Mr. Blank does not join in, since he already knew
the punch line, he nevertheless smiles at the man in the
black shirt, pleased with himself for having pulled off the
joke so well. When the hilarity at last dies down, the visitor looks at Mr. Blank and says: Do you know who I am?

I'm not sure, the old man replies. Not Fogg, in any
case. But there's no question that I've met you before—
many times, I think.

I'm your lawyer.

My lawyer. That's good . . . very good. I was hoping
I'd see you today. We have a lot to talk about.

Yes, says the man in the black shirt, patting the bundle
of files and folders on his lap. A great deal to talk about.
But before we get down to that, I want you to take a good
look at me and try to remember my name.

Mr. Blank looks carefully at the man's thin, angular
face, peers into his large gray eyes, studies his jaw and
forehead and mouth, but in the end he can do no more
than let out a sigh and shake his head in defeat.

I'm Quinn, Mr. Blank, the man says. Daniel Quinn.
Your first operative.

Mr. Blank groans. He is mortified with shame, embarrassed to such a point that a part of him, the innermost part of him, wants to crawl into a hole and die. Please forgive me, he says. My dear Quinn—my brother, my comrade, my loyal friend. It's these rotten pills I've been swallowing. They've screwed up my head, and I can't tell if I'm coming or going anymore.

You sent me on more missions than anyone else, Quinn says. Do you remember the Stillman case?

A little, Mr. Blank replies. Peter Stillman. Junior and Senior, if I'm not mistaken. One of them wore white clothes. I forget which now, but I think it was the son.

Exactly right. The son. And then there was that strange business with Fanshawe.

Sophie's first husband. The madman who disappeared.

Right again. But we mustn't forget the passport either. A small point, I suppose, but it was tough work just the same.

What passport?

My passport. The one that Anna Blume found when you sent her on her mission.

Anna? Do you know Anna?

Of course. Everyone knows Anna. She's something of a legend around here.

She deserves to be. There's no woman like her in the world.

And then, last but not least, there was my aunt, Molly Fitzsimmons, the woman who married Walt Rawley. I helped him write his memoirs.

Walt who?

Rawley. Once known as Walt the Wonder Boy.

Ah, yes. That was a long time ago, wasn't it?

Correct. A very long time ago.

And then?

That's it. You retired me after that.

Why would I do such a thing? What was I thinking?

I'd put in all those years, and the time came for me to go. Operatives don't last forever. It's the nature of the business.

When was that?

Nineteen ninety-three.

And what year is it now?

Two thousand and five.

Twelve years. What have you been doing with yourself since . . . since I retired you?

Traveling, mostly. By now, I've visited nearly every country in the world.

And now you're back, working as my lawyer. I'm glad it's you, Quinn. I always felt I could trust you.

You can, Mr. Blank. That's why I was given the job. Because we go so far back together.

You have to get me out of here. I don't think I can take it anymore.

That won't be easy. So many charges have been filed against you, I'm drowning in paperwork. You have to be patient. I wish I could give you an answer, but I have no idea how long it will take to sort things out.

Charges? What kind of charges?

The whole gamut, I'm afraid. From criminal indifference to sexual molestation. From conspiracy to commit fraud to negligent homicide. From defamation of character to first-degree murder. Shall I go on?

But I'm innocent. I've never done any of those things.

That's a debatable point. It all depends on how you look at it.

And what happens if we lose?

The nature of the punishment is still open to question. One group is advocating clemency, an across-the-board pardon on every count. But others are out for blood. And not just one or two of them. There's a whole gang, and they're becoming more and more vociferous.

Blood. I don't understand. You mean blood as in *death*?

Instead of answering, Quinn reaches into the pocket of his black shirt and pulls out a piece of paper, which he then unfolds in order to share what is written on it with Mr. Blank.

There was a meeting just two hours ago, Quinn says. I don't want to scare you, but someone got up and actually proposed this as a possible solution. I quote: *He shall be drawn through the streets to the place of his execution, there to be hanged and cut down alive, and his body shall be opened, his heart and bowels plucked out, and his privy members cut off and thrown into the fire before his eyes. Then his head shall be stricken off from his body, and his body shall be divided into four quarters, to be disposed of at our discretion.*

Lovely, Mr. Blank sighs. And what gentle soul came up with that plan?

It doesn't matter, Quinn says. I just want you to get a sense of what we're dealing with. I'll fight for you to the bitter end, but we have to be realistic. The way it looks now, we're probably going to have to work out some compromises.

It was Flood, wasn't it? Mr. Blank asks. That odious little man who came in here and insulted me this morning.

No, as a matter of fact it wasn't Flood, but that doesn't mean he isn't a dangerous person. You were very wise to refuse his invitation to go to the park. Later on, we discovered that he'd concealed a knife in his jacket. Once he got you out of the room, he was planning to kill you.

Ah. I figured as much. That lousy, good-for-nothing piece of shit.

I know it's hard being cooped up in this room, but I would suggest you stay here, Mr. Blank. If someone else invites you out for a walk in the park, invent some excuse and say no.

So there really is a park?

Yes, there really is a park.

And the birds. Are they in my head, or can I really hear them?

What kind of birds?

Crows or seagulls, I can't tell which.

Seagulls.

Then we must be near the ocean.

You picked the spot yourself. In spite of everything that's been going on here, you've gathered us all in a beautiful place. I'm thankful to you for that.

Then why don't you let me see it? I can't even open the goddamned window.

It's for your own protection. You wanted to be on the top floor, but we can't take any chances, can we?

I'm not going to commit suicide, if that's what you mean.

I know that. But not everyone shares my opinion.

Another one of your compromises, huh?

By way of response, Quinn shrugs his shoulders, glances down, and looks at his watch.

Time is running short, he says. I've brought along the files of one case, and I think we should get to it now. Unless you're feeling too tired, of course. If you prefer, I could always come back tomorrow.

No, no, Mr. Blank answers, waving his arm in disgust. Let's get it over with now.

Quinn opens the top folder and removes four eight-by-ten black-and-white photographs. Wheeling himself forward in the chair, he hands them to Mr. Blank and says: Benjamin Sachs. Does the name ring any bells?

I think so, the old man replies, but I'm not sure.

It's a bad one. One of the worst, as a matter of fact, but if we can mount a compelling defense against this charge, we might be able to set a precedent for the others. Do you follow me, Mr. Blank?

Mr. Blank nods in silence, already beginning to look through the pictures. The first one shows a tall, gangly man of about forty, perched on the railing of a fire escape in what appears to be Brooklyn, New York, looking out into the night in front of him—but then Mr. Blank moves on to the second photo, and suddenly that same man has lost his grip on the railing and is falling through the darkness, a silhouette of splayed limbs caught in midair, plunging toward the ground below. That is disturbing enough, but once Mr. Blank comes to the third picture, a shudder of recognition passes through him. The tall man is on a dirt road somewhere out in the country, and he is swinging a metal softball bat at a bearded man who is standing in front of him. The image is frozen at the precise instant the bat makes contact with the bearded man's head, and from the look on his face it is clear that the blow will kill him, that within a matter of seconds he will fall to the ground with his skull crushed as blood pours from the wound and gathers in a puddle around his corpse.

Mr. Blank clutches his face, tearing at the skin with his fingers. He is finding it difficult to breathe now, for he already knows the subject of the fourth picture, even if he can't remember how or why he knows it, and because he can anticipate the explosion of the homemade bomb that will tear the tall man apart and cast his mangled body to the four winds, he does not have the strength to look at it. Instead, he lets the four photographs slip out of his hands and fall to the floor, and then, bringing those same hands up to his face, he covers his eyes and begins to weep.

◆ ◆ ◆

NOW QUINN IS GONE, and once again Mr. Blank is alone in
the room, sitting at the desk with the ballpoint pen in his
right hand. The onrush of tears stopped more than twenty
minutes ago, and as he opens the pad and turns to the second page, he says to himself: I was only doing my job. If
things turned out badly, the report still had to be written,
and I can't be blamed for telling the truth, can I? Then,
applying himself to the task at hand, he adds three more
names to his list:

> John Trause
> Sophie
> Daniel Quinn
> Marco Fogg
> Benjamin Sachs

Mr. Blank puts down the pen, closes the pad, and
pushes both articles aside. He realizes now that he was
hoping for a visit from Fogg, the man with all the funny
stories, but even though there is no clock in the room and
no watch on his wrist, meaning that he has no idea of the
time, not even an approximate one, he senses that the
hour for tea and light conversation has passed. Perhaps,
before long, Anna will be coming back to serve him dinner, and if by chance it isn't Anna who comes, but another woman or man sent in as a substitute, then he
means to protest, to misbehave, to rant and shout, to
cause such a ruckus that it will blow the very roof clear
into the sky.

For want of anything better to do just now, Mr. Blank
decides to go on with his reading. Directly below
Trause's story about Sigmund Graf and the Confederation
there is a longer manuscript of some one hundred and
forty pages, which, unlike the previous work, comes with

a cover page that announces the title of the piece and the author's name:

Travels in the Scriptorium
by
N. R. Fanshawe

Aha, Mr. Blank says out loud. That's more like it. Maybe we're finally getting somewhere, after all.

Then he turns to the first page and begins to read:

The old man sits on the edge of the narrow bed, palms spread out on his knees, head down, staring at the floor. He has no idea that a camera is planted in the ceiling directly above him. The shutter clicks silently once every second, producing eighty-six thousand four hundred still photos with each revolution of the earth. Even if he knew he was being watched, it wouldn't make any difference. His mind is elsewhere, stranded among the figments in his head as he searches for an answer to the question that haunts him.

Who is he? What is he doing here? When did he arrive and how long will he remain? With any luck, time will tell us all. For the moment, our only task is to study the pictures as attentively as we can and refrain from drawing any premature conclusions.

There are a number of objects in the room, and on each one a strip of white tape has been affixed to the surface, bearing a single word written out in block letters. On the bedside table, for example, the word is TABLE. On the lamp, the word is LAMP. Even on the wall, which is not strictly speaking an object, there is a strip of tape that reads WALL. The old man looks up for a moment, sees the wall, sees the strip of tape attached to the wall, and pronounces the word *wall* in a soft voice. What cannot be known at this point is whether he is reading the word on the strip of tape or simply referring to the wall itself. It could be that he has forgotten how to read but still recognizes things for what they are and can call them by their names, or, conversely, that he has lost the ability to recognize things for what they are but still knows how to read.

He is dressed in blue-and-yellow striped cotton pajamas, and his feet are encased in a pair of black leather slippers. It is unclear to him exactly where he is. In the room, yes, but in what building is the room located? In a house? In a hospital? In a prison? He can't remember how long he has been here or the nature of the circumstances that precipitated his removal to this place. Perhaps he has always been here; perhaps this is where he has lived since the day he was born. What he knows is that his heart is filled with an implacable sense of guilt. At the same time, he can't escape the feeling that he is the victim of a terrible injustice.

There is one window in the room, but the shade is drawn, and as far as he can remember he has not yet looked out of it. Likewise with the door and its white porcelain knob. Is he locked in, or is he free to come and go as he wishes? He has yet to investigate this matter— for, as stated in the first paragraph above, his mind is elsewhere, adrift in the past as he wanders among the phantom beings that clutter his head, struggling to answer the question that haunts him.

The pictures do not lie, but neither do they tell the whole story. They are merely a record of time passing, the outward evidence. The old man's age, for example, is difficult to determine from the slightly out-of-focus black-and-white images. The only fact that can be set down with any certainty is that he is not young, but the word *old* is a flexible term and can be used to describe a person anywhere between sixty and a hundred. We will therefore drop the epithet *old man* and henceforth refer to the person in the room as Mr. Blank. For the time being, no first name will be necessary.

Mr. Blank stands up from the bed at last, pauses briefly to steady his balance, and then shuffles over to the desk at the other end of the room. He feels tired, as if he has just woken from a fitful, too short night of sleep, and as the soles of his slippers scrape along the bare wood floor, he is reminded of the sound of sandpaper. Far off in the distance, beyond the room, beyond the building in which the room is located, he hears the faint cry of a bird—perhaps a crow, perhaps a seagull, he can't tell which . . .

BY NOW, MR. BLANK has read all he can stomach, and he is not the least bit amused. In an outburst of pent-up anger and frustration, he tosses the manuscript over his shoulder with a violent flick of the wrist, not even bothering to turn around to see where it lands. As it flutters through the air and then thuds to the floor behind him, he pounds his fist on the desk and says in a loud voice: When is this nonsense going to end?

IT WILL NEVER END. For Mr. Blank is one of us now, and struggle though he might to understand his predicament, he will always be lost. I believe I speak for all his charges when I say he is getting what he deserves—no more, no less. Not as a form of punishment, but as an act of supreme justice and compassion. Without him, we are nothing, but the paradox is that we, the figments of another mind, will outlive the mind that made us, for once we are thrown into the world, we continue to exist forever, and our stories go on being told, even after we are dead.

Mr. Blank might have acted cruelly toward some of his charges over the years, but not one of us thinks he hasn't done everything in his power to serve us well. That is why I plan to keep him where he is. The room is his world now, and the longer the treatment goes on, the more he will come to accept the generosity of what has been done for him. Mr. Blank is old and enfeebled, but as long as he remains in the room with the shuttered window and the locked door, he can never die, never disappear, never be anything but the words I am writing on his page.

In a short while, a woman will enter the room and feed him his dinner. I haven't yet decided who that woman will be, but if all goes well between now and then, I will send in Anna. That will make Mr. Blank happy, and when all is said and done, he has probably suffered enough for one day. Anna will feed Mr. Blank his dinner, then wash him and put him to bed. Mr. Blank will lie awake in the dark for some time, listening to the cries of birds in the far distance, but then his eyes will at last grow heavy, and his lids will close. He will fall asleep, and when he wakes up in the morning, the treatment will begin again. But for now it is still the day it has always been since the first word of this report, and now is the moment when Anna kisses Mr. Blank on the cheek and tucks him in, and now is the moment when she stands up from the bed and begins walking toward the door. Sleep well, Mr. Blank.

Lights out.